完全

莫非定律

The Complete Murphy's Law

書林

完全莫非定律

The Complete Murphy's Law

Arthur Bloch 著

林為正 譯

書林

國家圖書館出版品預行編目資料

完全莫非定律 The Complete Murphy's Law ／ Arthur
Bloch 著；林爲正譯 －－ 三版 ．－－
臺北市：書林，2005〔民 94〕
　　　面；公分．－－（英文叢書 74）
　　　中英對照
　　　ISBN: 957-445-110-0（平裝）

1. 英國語言 － 讀本

874.6　　　　　　　　　　　　　94017312

英語叢書 74

完全莫非定律
The Complete Murphy's Law

著　　　者	Arthur Bloch	
譯　　　者	林為正	
編　　　輯	周佩蓉	
校　　　對	黃嘉音・王建文・Lynn Sauvé	
出　版　者	書林出版有限公司	
	100 台北市羅斯福路 4 段 60 號 3 樓	
	電話 02-2368-4938・02-2365-8617 傳真 02-2368-8929・02-2363-6630	
台北書林書店	106 台北市新生南路三段 88 號 2 樓之 5	TEL: 02-2365-8617
北 區 業 務 部	100 台北市羅斯福路四段 60 號 3 樓	TEL: 02-2368-7226
中 區 業 務 部	403 台中市五權路 2 之 143 號 6 樓	TEL: 04-2376-3799
南 區 業 務 部	802 高雄市五福一路 77 號 2 樓之 1	TEL: 07-229-0300
發　行　人	蘇正隆	
出 版 經 理	蘇恆隆	
郵　　　撥	15743873・書林出版有限公司	
網　　　址	http://www.bookman.com.tw	
經 銷 代 理	紅螞蟻圖書有限公司	
	台北市內湖區舊宗路 2 段 121 巷 28 號 4 樓	
	電話 02-2795-3656(代表號) 傳真 02-2795-4100	
登　記　證	局版臺業字第一八三一號	
出 版 日 期	2005 年 11 月三版一刷，2010 年 9 月三刷	
定　　　價	260 元	
I　S　B　N	957-445-110-0	

目錄
Contents

INTRODUCTION
前 言

Have you ever received a phone call the minute you sat down on the toilet? Has the bus you were waiting for ever appeared the instant you lit up a cigarette? Has it ever rained the day you washed your car, or stopped raining just after you bought an umbrella? Perhaps you realized at the time that something was afoot, that some universal principle was just out of your grasp, itching to be called by name. Or perhaps, having heard of Murphy's Law, the Peter Principle, or the Law of Selective Gravity, you have wanted to invoke one of these, only to find that you have forgotten its exact wording.

Here, then, is the first complete reference book of the wit and wisdom of our most delightfully demented technologists, bureaucrats, humanists, and antisocial observers, prepared and presented with the purpose of providing us all with a little Karmic Relief. The listing has been made as definitive as possible. In researching these interdisciplinary tenets, we found numerous redundancies (which verify the validity of the observations), frequent conflicting claims to authorship, and scores of anonymous donations. We are forced to acknowledge the contribution of the inimitable Zymurgy who said, " Once you open a can of worms, the only way to recan them is to use a larger can." By applying this Murphic morsel to the present volume, we come to realize that this project, once undertaken, has grown in size and scope as further principles, new and old, have been revealed by our beacon of truth.

Throughout history pundits and poseurs have regaled us with the laws of the universe, the subtle yet immutable substructure that is the basis of cosmic order. From people of religion we have

　　你曾不曾才坐上馬桶電話就來？才點菸你的公車就到？才洗車就下雨，才買傘雨就停？也許當時你明白，冥冥之中有個無所不在的原理在運轉，非人力所能左右，教人恨不能有個名堂加以稱呼。也許你已經聽過莫非定律、某某原則、選擇性重力等說法，想引述時才發現自己忘了確切的遣詞用字。

　　本書破天荒完整蒐羅了瘋癲成趣的科技人員、政府官員、人文學家、社會觀察家的機智與智慧，編纂方式力求人人都能樂在其中，條列方式則盡可能明確。蒐尋這些跨學科的原則時，我們發現有許多是一說再說的（這也證明這些心得不假），也常遇到出處有爭議的，還有不少佚名撰稿人。我們不得不承認無法模仿的Zymurgy先生所投的那則：

　　「蟲罐子一旦打開，只有用更大的罐子才裝得回去。」

　　把這則莫非小品應用到本書，我們便明白，編纂工作一旦展開，厚度與廣度會一再增加，因為真理之光照出了更多有新有舊的原則。

　　從古到今，學者雅士早為我們找出許多宇宙的定律，隱而不移的內在結構，也就是宇宙秩序的奠基石。從宗教家那裡，我們得到了道德定律；從神秘主義者那裡得到命運定律；從理性主義者那裡得到理則模式定律；從藝術家那裡得到美學定律。如今輪到科技專家來引導世人的視聽。

　　科技與科學所走的一貫路線是絕望。如果你不以為然，看看Ginsberg的定理（theorem）不就是熱力學的另一個版本：1.你贏不了，2.你沒辦法扯平，3.你不想玩都不行。宇宙就像一只巨大的燉鍋，兀自熬了四十億年。總有一天誰也分不出哪個是紅蘿蔔，那個是洋蔥。

　　「那麼，短期的事情、眾所皆知的封閉系統又如何呢？」你可

received the Moral Laws; from mystics, the Laws of Karma; from rationalists, the Laws of Logical Form; and from artists, the Laws of Aesthetics. Now it is the technologists' turn to bend our collective ear.

The official party line of technology, of science itself, is despair. If you doubt this, witness the laws of thermodynamics as they are restated in Ginsberg's Theorem: 1. You can't win; 2. You can't break even; 3. You can't even quit the game. The universe is simmering down, like a giant stew left to cook for four billion years. Sooner or later we won't be able to tell the carrots from the onions.

"But what of the short run, the proverbial closed system?" you may well ask as you sit gazing out of your penthouse window, sipping your vodka martini and watching the hustling throngs of God's little creatures going about their business. Alas, we've only to look at this business, as exemplified in the good bureaucracy, through the eyes of Peter, Parkinson, et al. We will realize that it is only a matter of time before the microcosmic specks we call big business and government, like their universal counterpart, lose their ability to succeed in spite of themselves.

"We are on the wrong side of the tapestry," said Father Brown, G. K. Chesterton's famous clerical sleuth. And indeed we are. A few loose ends, an occasional thread, are all we ever see of the great celestial masterwork of the most expensive carpet weaver of them all. A small number of courageous individuals have dared to explore the far side of the tapestry, have braved the wrath of the Keeper of the Rug in their search for truth. It is to these individuals that this volume is dedicated.

能這麼自問，從閣樓窗戶向外凝望，啜著雞尾酒，看著一群群上帝創造的小生物熙熙攘攘忙著自己的事情。唉，我們只需透過 Peter、Parkinson 等這些人的眼睛來看看這些事物，像是良好的官僚體系，我們自然會明白這些我們稱之爲大企業和政府的小沙粒，總有一天也會像宇宙裡對等的部分一樣，除了苟延殘喘，一無是處。

「我們站的位置是繡毯的反面。」布朗神父（Father Brown）這麼說，他是英國作家 G. K. Chesterton 著名的文字偵探。這是實情。那位最昂貴的織毯者所製的偉大宇宙之毯，我們只能驚鴻一瞥，瞄到三兩條線。少數勇者敢探索地毯的另一面，甘冒觸怒這位守毯者之險以追尋眞理。本書謹獻給這些勇者。

MURPHOLOGY
莫非學

MURPHY'S LAW:

If anything can go wrong, it will.

Corollaries:

1. Nothing is as easy as it looks.
2. Everything takes longer than you think.
3. If there is a possibility of several things going wrong, the one that will cause the most damage will be the one to go wrong.
4. If you perceive that there are four possible ways in which a procedure can go wrong, and circumvent these, then a fifth way will promptly develop.
5. Left to themselves, things tend to go from bad to worse.
6. Whenever you set out to do something, something else must be done first.
7. Every solution breeds new problems.
8. It is impossible to make anything foolproof because fools are so ingenious.
9. Mother nature is a bitch.

BENEDICT'S PRINCIPLE (formerly Murphy' Ninth Corollary):

Nature always sides with the hidden flaw.

LAW OF REVELATION:

The hidden flaw never remains hidden.

THE MURPHY'S PHILOSOPHY:

Smile. Tomorrow will be worse.

MURPHY'S CONSTANT:

Matter will be damaged in direct proportion to its value.

▼莫非定律：

會出錯的事，一定出錯。

▼同理可證：

1. 凡事做起來都比看起來難。
2. 凡事做起來都比你以為的來得久。
3. 如果有幾件事可能出錯，出錯的一定是傷害性最大的那件。
4. 如果你察覺某個流程有四個破綻，也都防範了，第五個破綻馬上就會出現。
5. 事情任其發展只會愈來愈糟。
6. 不管你想著手做什麼事，一定有別的得先做完。
7. 解決方案都會帶來新的問題。
8. 傻事防不勝防，誰教傻子總是想得出新傻法。
9. 大自然只會給人添麻煩。

▼Benedict 的原則（以前是第九條莫非的同理可證）

大自然總是助長隱藏的缺陷。

▼揭發定律：

隱藏的缺陷遲早會見光。

▼莫非人生觀：

能笑就笑。明天會更糟。

▼莫非定理：

東西愈重要，就壞得愈嚴重。

QUANTIZATION REVISION OF MURPHY'S LAW:

1. If we lose much by having things go wrong, take all possible care.
2. If we have nothing to lose by change, relax.
3. If we have everything to gain by change, relax.
4. If it doesn't matter, it does not matter.

LOFTA'S LAMENT:

Nobody can leave well enough alone.

O'TOOLE'S COMMENTARY ON MURPHY'S LAW:

Murphy was an optimist.

ZYMURGY'S SEVENTH EXCEPTION TO MURPHY'S LAW:

When it rains, it pours.

BOLING'S POSTULATE:

If you're feeling good, don't worry. You'll get over it.

CHRIS'S COMMENT:

You always have to give up something you want for something you want more.

WHITE'S STATEMENT:

Don't lose heart.

Owen's Commentary On White's Statement:

They might want to cut it out.

Byrd's Addition To Owen's Commentary On White's Statement:

And they want to avoid a lengthy search.

ILES' LAW:

There is always an easier way to do it.

▼莫非定律的限制修訂：
　1. 事情出錯就會損失慘重的話，盡可能小心。
　2. 事情變卦沒有損失，就不用著急。
　3. 事情變卦有利無害，也不用著急。
　4. 可有可無，那就是可無。

▼Lofta 的悲哀：
　誰也無法不管閒事。

▼O'Toole 對莫非定律的評語：
　莫非生性樂觀。

▼Zymurgy 對莫非定律的第七條例外補充：
　雨不下則已，下必傾盆。

▼Boling 的前題：
　心情好沒什麼，放心好了，待會就沒感覺了。

▼Chris 的看法：
　想得到熊掌，總是有魚得放棄。

▼White 的說法：
　別失去信心。

▼Owen 評 White 的說法：
　人家說不定想把它去掉。

▼Byrd 補充 Owen 評 White 的說法：
　再說人家可不想花時間找回來。

▼Iles 的定律：
　方法總是有更簡單的。

◥ Corollaries:

1. When looking directly at the easier way, especially for long periods, you will not see it.
2. Neither will Iles.

◥ HEYMANN'S LAW:

Mediocrity imitates.

◥ CHISHOLM'S FIRST LAW:

When things are going well, something will go wrong.

◥ Corollaries:

1. When things just can't get any worse, they will.
2. Anytime things appear to be going better, you have overlooked something.

◥ CHISHOLM'S SECOND LAW:

Proposals, as understood by the proposer, will be judged otherwise by others.

◥同理可證：

  1. 要是你直接找那個更簡單的方法，你一定找不到，找愈久愈找
    不到。

  2. 連 Iles 也找不到。

◥Heymann 的定律：

  庸人專事模仿。

◥Chisholm 的第一定律：

  每當一切順利就會出紕漏。

◥同理可證：

  1. 情況要是糟得不能再糟了，就還會再更糟。

  2. 要是一切看來順利，一定哪兒疏忽了。

◥Chisholm 的第二定律：

  任何建議總是提的人是什麼意思，聽的人就想
  成別的意思。

完全莫非定律

◥Corollaries:

1. If you explain something so clearly that nobody can misunderstand, somebody will.
2. If you do something which you are sure will meet with everybody's approval, somebody won't like it.
3. Procedures devised to implement the purpose won't quite work.

◥LAW OF THE LIE:

No matter how often a lie is shown to be false, there will remain a percentage of people who believe it true.

◥SCOTT'S FIRST LAW:

No matter what goes wrong, it will probably look right.

◥SCOTT'S SECOND LAW:

When an error has been detected and corrected, it will be found to have been correct in the first place.

◥Corollary:

After the correction has been found in error, it will be impossible to fit the original quantity back into the equation.

◥GUMPERSON'S LAW:

The probability of anything happening is in inverse ratio to its desirability.

◥ISSAWI'S LAWS OF PROGRESS:

The Course of Progress:

Most things get steadily worse.

The Path of Progress:

A shortcut is the longest distance between two points.

▼同理可證：

　　1. 就算你把事情說得一清二楚，就是有人會不清楚。

　　2. 就算你有把握把事情辦得皆大歡喜，一定有人會不喜歡。

　　3. 專為達成目的所安排的程序，就是會不如人意。

▼謊話定律：

　　謊話不管給人揭穿多少次，總是會有些人信以為眞。

▼Scott 的第一定律：

　　不管出的是什麼錯，看起來八成都對。

▼Scott 的第二定律：

　　每當查出錯誤並更正之後，才發現原先就是對的。

▼同理可證：

　　發現改錯了，原先的數量卻怎麼也代不回方程式裡頭去。

▼Gumperson 的定律：

　　事情發生的機率，與人們希望該事發生的期待成反比。

▼Issawi 的進步定律：

　　進步的歷程：

　　事情大半一天不如一天。

　　進步的路徑：

　　捷徑是兩點間最遠的距離。

The Dialectics of Progress:

Direct action produces direct reaction.

The Pace of Progress:

Society is a mule, not a car. If pressed too hard, it will kick and throw off its rider.

SODD'S FIRST LAW:

When a person attempts a task, he or she will be thwarted in that task by the unconscious intervention of some other presence (animate or inanimate). Nevertheless, some tasks are completed, since the intervening presence is itself attempting a task and is, of course, subject to interference.

SODD'S SECOND LAW:

Sooner or later, the worse possible set of circumstances is bound to occur.

Corollary:

Any system must be designed to withstand the worst possible set of circumstances.

SIMON'S LAW:

Everything put together falls apart sooner or later.

GEORGE'S LAW:

All pluses have their minuses.

ARISTOTLE'S DICTUM:

One should always prefer the probable impossible to the improbable possible.

進步的辯證法：

直接行動帶來直接反應。

進步的速度：

社會是頭騾子，不是車子。把牠逼急了，牠會把騎士摔下騾背。

▼Sodd 的第一定律：

不管做什麼事，一定有人、事、物在場阻擾。不過有些事情還是順利完成，因為阻擾本身也是一件進行中的事，所以自然也會受到阻擾。

▼Sodd 的第二定律：

最不湊巧的事遲早會湊在一起。

▼同理可證：

任何系統都要為應付最壞的情況設計。

▼Simon 的定律：

整理好的東西遲早會變亂。

▼George 的定律：

有利必有弊。

▼亞里斯多德（希臘哲學家）的格言：

寧可選合理的難事，也不可選不合理的易事。

RUDIN'S LAW:

In crises that force people to choose among alternative courses of action, most people will choose the worst one possible.

GINSBERG'S THEOREM:

1. You can't win.
2. You can't break even.
3. You can't even quit the game.

FREEMAN'S COMMENTARY ON GINSBERG'S THEOREM:

Every major philosophy that attempts to make life seem meaningful is based on the negation of one part of Ginsberg's Theorem. To wit:

1. Capitalism is based on the assumption that you can win.
2. Socialism is based on the assumption that you can break even.
3. Mysticism is based on the assumption that you can quit the game.

EHRMAN'S COMMENTARY:

1. Things will get worse before they get better.
2. Who said things would get better?

EVERITT'S LAW OF THERMODYNAMICS:

Confusion is always increasing in society. Only if someone or something works extremely hard can this confusion be reduced to order in a limited region. Nevertheless, this effort will still result in an increase in the total confusion of society at large.

BOBBY'S BELIEF:

Confusion not only reigns, it pours.

◤Rudin 的定律：

一般人面臨危機而只有幾條路可走的話，大半就會挑上那條最差的路走。

◤Ginsberg 的理論：

1. 你贏不了。
2. 你沒辦法扯平。
3. 你想撒手不玩都不行。

◤Freeman 補充 Ginsberg 的理論：

賦予人生意義的大哲學體系，都是以 Ginsberg 理論的反面做基礎。如下：

1. 資本主義的基本前提是你贏得了。
2. 社會主義的基本前提是你能扯平。
3. 神秘主義的基本前提是你可以撒手不玩。

◤Ehrman 的評語：

1. 事情還來不及好轉就會惡化。
2. 誰說會好轉來著？

◤Everitt 的熱力學定律：

社會的亂象總是與日俱增。唯有某人、某事發揮了無比的作用，才能在小範圍內化混亂為秩序。只可惜這個力量依然會多添一樁社會的混亂。

◤Bobby 的信條：

天下何止亂，是大亂。

 完全莫非定律

MURPHY'S LAW OF THERMODYNAMICS:

Things get worse under pressure.

LUNSFORD'S RULE OF SCIENTIFIC ENDEAVOR:

The simple explanation always follows the complex solution.

RUDNICKI'S NOBEL PRINCIPLE:

Only someone who understands something absolutely can explain it so no one else can understand it.

COMMONER'S LAW OF ECOLOGY:

Nothing ever goes away.

PUDDER'S LAW:

Anything that begins well, ends badly.
Anything that begins badly, ends worse.

STOCKMAYER'S THEOREM:

If it looks easy, it's tough.
If it looks tough, it's damn well impossible.

WYNNE'S LAW:

Negative slack tends to increase.

TYLCZAK'S PROBABILITY POSTULATE:

Random events tend to occur in groups.

ZYMURGY'S LAW OF EVOLVING SYSTEMS DYNAMICS:

Once you open a can of worms, the only way to recan them is to use a larger can.

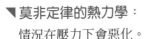

▼莫非定律的熱力學：
情況在壓力下會惡化。

▼Lunsford 的科學嘗試法則：
解釋簡單，解決一定複雜。

▼Rudnicki 的最高原則：
凡事唯有徹底了解的人才能解釋得了，但除了他自己，誰也聽不懂。

▼平民的環保定律：
物質不滅——怎麼甩也甩不掉。

▼Pudder 的定律：
開始的時候好，結束就壞。
開始的時候壞，結束會更糟。

▼Stockmayer 的定理：
看起來簡單的其實難。
看起來難的，根本就是不可能。

▼Wynne 的定律：
紕漏只增不減。

▼Tylczak 的機率原則：
隨機發生的事都不約而同出現。

▼Zymurgy 的進化體系力學的定律：
蟲罐子一旦打開，只有用更大的罐子才裝得回去。

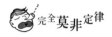

◥KAISER'S COMMENT ON ZYMURGY:

Never open a can of worms unless you plan to go fishing.

◥STURGEON'S LAW:

Ninety percent of everything is crud.

◥NON-RECIPROCAL LAWS OF EXPECTATIONS:

Negative expectations yield negative results.

Positive expectations yield negative results.

◥LAW OF REGRESSIVE ACHIEVEMENT:

Last year's was always better.

◥THE UNSPEAKABLE LAW:

As soon as you mention something

—if it's good, it goes away.

—if it's bad, it happens.

▼Kaiser 評 Zymurgy 的定律：
如果不釣魚就別開蟲罐子。

▼Sturgeon 的定律：
任何事物都有九成是多餘的。

▼反之不然的期望定律：
想到壞事，壞事就發生。
想到好事，發生的還是壞事。

▼退步定律：
今不如昔。

▼少說為妙的定律：
每當你提到某事
——好的就告吹。
——壞的就降臨。

APPLIED MURPHOLOGY
應用莫非學

◥BOOKER'S LAW:

An ounce of application is worth a ton of abstraction.

◥KLIPSTEIN'S LAWS:

Applied to General Engineering:

1. A patent application will be preceded by a similar application submitted one week earlier by an independent worker.
2. Firmness of delivery dates is inversely proportional to the tightness of the schedule.
3. Dimensions will always be expressed in the least usable term. Velocity, for example, will be expressed in furlongs per fortnight.
4. Any wire cut to length will be too short.

Applied to Prototyping and Production:

1. Tolerances will accumulate unidirectionally toward maximum difficulty to assemble.
2. If a project requires "n" components, there will be "n-1" units in stock.
3. A motor will rotate in the wrong direction.
4. A fail-safe circuit will destroy others.
5. A transistor protected by a fast-acting fuse will protect the fuse by blowing first.
6. A failure will not appear until a unit has passed final inspection.
7. A purchased component or instrument will meet its specs long enough, and only long enough, to pass incoming inspection.
8. After the last of sixteen mounting screws has been removed from an access cover, it will be discovered that the wrong access cover has been removed.
9. After an access cover has been secured by sixteen hold-down screws, it will be discovered that the gasket has been omitted.

◥Booker 的定律：

一盎斯的應用勝過一噸的理論。

◥Klipstein 的定律：

應用於一般事業：

1. 申請專利時一定會發現，有個獨立工作室已經在一週前提出類似的申請案了。

2. 交件的準時程度與時間表的緊迫程度成反比。

3. 長寬高總以最罕用的單位註明。舉個例吧，速度會說成每兩個星期若干哇長（相當於220碼）。

4. 依尺寸剪的電線一定短一截。

應用於模型製作與生產：

1. 誤差會讓裝配變得更為困難。

2. 如果某方案需要 n 個配件，庫房裡頭一定只有 n − 1 個。

3. 馬達總是轉錯方向。

4. 有保護裝置的電路會把別的電路燒壞。

5. 以靈敏的保險絲保護的電晶體，會為了保護保險絲而先燒壞。

6. 通過最後一關檢查，瑕疵才會出現。

7. 訂購的零件或器材符合設計說明書的時間，只到通過檢驗那天。

8. 入口蓋的十六個固定螺絲釘全都卸了下來之後，才知道卸錯蓋子了。

9. 入口蓋用十六個固定螺絲釘安裝好了，才發現防漏墊沒裝。

 完全莫非定律

10. After an instrument has been assembled, extra components will be found on the bench.

PATTISON'S LAW OF ELECTRONICS:
If wires can be connected in two different ways, the first way blows the fuse.

FARRELL'S LAW OF NEWFANGLED GADGETRY:
The most expensive component is the one that breaks.

THE RECOMMENDED PRACTICES COMMITTEE OF THE INTERNATIONAL SOCIETY OF PHILOSOPHICAL ENGINEERS' UNIVERSAL LAWS FOR NAIVE ENGINEERS:

1. In any calculation, any error that can creep in will do so.
2. Any error in any calculation will be in the direction of most harm.
3. In any formula, constants (especially those obtained from engineering handbooks) are to be treated as variables.
4. The best approximation of service conditions in the laboratory will not begin to meet those conditions encountered in actual service.
5. The most vital dimension on any plan or drawing stands the greatest chance of being omitted.
6. If only one bid can be secured on any project, the price will be unreasonable.
7. If a test installation functions perfectly, all subsequent production units will malfunction.
8. All delivery promises must be multiplied by a factor of 2.0.
9. Major changes in construction will always be requested after fabrication is nearly completed.

10. 設備裝配好了，才發現工作台上還有零件。

▼Pattison 的電子定律：

如果線路有兩種接法，先試的一種會燒掉保險絲。

▼Farrell 的新奇設備定律：

故障的零件會是最貴的那個。

▼國際老鳥工程師協會的委員會給菜鳥工程師的放諸四海皆準
定律：

1. 計算裡會出的任何錯誤都會出現。

2. 計算裡出的錯一定帶來最大的傷害。

3. 任何公式裡的常數（特別是從工程手冊上查來的），必須當做變
   數來用。

4. 實驗室裡逼真的假設狀況，一點都不符合實際狀況。

5. 計畫或藍圖裡最重要的層面，最有可能漏掉。

6. 投標案裡要是只有一個標可投，價格一定離譜。

7. 如果試車運作良好，底下的生產單位都會出問題。

8. 一切說好的送貨時間都得乘上係數 2.0。

9. 房子快蓋好了，人家才會要求做大幅結構更動。

10. Parts that positively cannot be assembled in improper order will be.

11. Interchangeable parts won't.

12. Manufacturer's specifications of performance should be multiplied by a factor of 0.5.

13. Salespeople's claims for performance should be multiplied by a factor of 0.25.

14. Installation and Operating Instructions shipped with the device will be promptly discarded by the Receiving Department.

15. Any device requiring service or adjustment will be least accessible.

16. Service Conditions as given on specifications will be exceeded.

17. If more than one person is responsible for a miscalculation, no one will be at fault.

18. Identical units that test in an identical fashion will not behave in an identical fashion in the field.

19. If, in engineering practice, a safety factor is set through service experience at an ultimate value, an ingenious idiot will promptly calculate a method to exceed said safety factor.

20. Warranty and guarantee clauses are voided by payment of the invoice.

HARPER'S MAGAZINE LAW:

You never find an article until you replace it.

RICHARD'S COMPLEMENTARY RULES OF OWNERSHIP:

1. If you keep anything long enough you can throw it away.

2. If you throw anything away, you will need it as soon as it is no longer accessible.

10. 非得按部就班裝配不可的零件，不必按部就班裝配也可以。

11. 可互換的零件千萬換不得。

12. 製造廠商列出的功能明細都得乘上係數0.5。

13. 行銷人員聲稱的功能都得乘上係數0.25。

14. 與設備一起送來的裝機操作說明，馬上就會給收貨部門丟掉。

15. 凡是需要維修或調整的裝置，都裝在最難接近的角落。

16. 規格上載明的運作限制一定被打破。

17. 如果計算誤差許多人都有責任，就找不出誰出錯。

18. 一模一樣的設備用一模一樣的方法測試後，到實際操作時反應卻各不相同。

19. 在工程實作裡，常會透過工作經驗設定一些最大值做為安全限度，只要來了個異想天開的白癡，一下子就能想出打破安全限度的方法。

20. 任何保證條文等貨款付清就失效。

▼哈潑雜誌定律：

文章總要在補上之後才會找到原來要的那篇。

▼Richard 對所有權條文之補充：

1. 東西只要在你手頭夠久，你就可以把它丟了。

2. 東西只要丟棄了，一旦找不回來時你就會需要它。

GILLETTE'S LAW OF HOUSEHOLD MOVING:

What you lost during your first move you find during your second move.

HEISENBERG'S UNCERTAINTY PRINCIPLE:

The location of all objects cannot be known simultaneously.

Corollary:

If a lost thing is found, something else will disappear.

O'BRIENS' OBSERVATION:

The quickest way to find something is to start looking for something else.

MARYANN'S LAW:

You can always find what you're not looking for.

ADVANCED LAW OF THE SEARCH:

The first place to look for anything is the last place you would expect to find it.

BOOB'S LAW:

You always find something in the last place you look.

BLOCH'S REBUTTAL TO BOOB'S LAW:

You always find something in the first place you look, but you never find it the first time you look there.

GLATUM'S LAW OF MATERIALISTIC ACQUISITIVENESS:

The perceived usefulness of an article is inversely proportional to its actual usefulness once bought and paid for.

◥Gillette 的搬家定律：

第一次搬家掉的東西，第二次搬家就會找到。

◥Heisenberg 的不確定原則：

東西放在哪，總是無法樣樣記得。

◥依理類推：

要是丟掉的東西又找回來，一定有別的東西會不見。

◥O'Brien 的心得：

找東西最快的方法就是找別的東西。

◥Maryann 的定律：

不想找的東西，一定找得到。

◥找東西的進階定律：

找東西要從最不可能的地方找起。

◥Boob 的定律：

失物會在你最後找的地方等你。

◥Bloch 對 Boob 的定律的反駁定律：

失物會在你第一次找的地方等你，只不過當時就是沒看到。

◥Glatum 的物質佔有慾定律：

東西在成交付款之後，原來看起來有多好用，
實際上就有多難用。

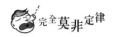

◥GILLETTE'S LAW OF TELEPHONE DYNAMICS:

The phone call you've been waiting for comes the minute you're out the door.

◥FRANK'S PHONE PHENOMENA:

If you have a pen, there's no paper.

If you have paper, there's no pen.

If you have both, there's no message.

◥WOLTER'S LAW:

If you have the time, you won't have the money.

If you have the money, you won't have the time.

◥Gillett 的電話動力學：
　　等半天的電話，才出門就打來。

◥Frank 的電話現象學：
　　有筆就沒紙。
　　有紙就沒筆。
　　紙筆都有就沒人留話。

◥Wolter 的定律：
　　有閒就沒錢。
　　有錢就沒閒。

ADVACED MURPHOLOGY
進階莫非學

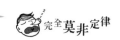

SCHNATTERLY'S SUMMING UP OF THE COROLLARIES:

If anything can't go wrong, it will.

SILVERMAN'S PARADOX:

If Murphy's Law can go wrong, it will.

THE EXTENDED MURPHY'S LAW:

If a series of events goes wrong, it will do so in the worst possible sequence.

FARNSDICK'S COROLLARY TO THE FIFTH COROLLARY:

After things have gone from bad to worse, the cycle will repeat itself.

GATTUSO'S EXTENSION OF MURPHY'S LAW:

Nothing is ever so bad that it can't get worse.

NAGLER'S COMMENT ON THE ORIGIN OF MURPHY'S LAW:

Murphy's Law was not propounded by Murphy, but by another man of the same name.

LYNCH'S LAW:

When the going gets tough, everyone leaves.

KOHN'S COROLLARY TO MURPHY'S LAW:

Two wrongs are only the beginning.

McDONALD'S COROLLARY TO MURPHY'S LAW:

In any given set of circumstances, the proper course of action is determined by subsequent events.

▼Schnatterly 總結同理可證：
　一切沒問題就會出問題。

▼Silverman 的弔詭：
　莫非定律要是會出錯，一定出錯。

▼引申莫非定律：
　如果出了一連串紕漏，一定是以最糟糕的順序排列。

▼Farnsdick 類推第五條同理可證：
　事情要是每下愈況，還會每下愈況。

▼Gattuso 引申的莫非定律：
　情況再糟糕，總是可以變得更糟。

▼Nagler 評莫非定律的起源：
　莫非定律不是莫非所創，是另一個同名同姓的人所創。

▼Lynch 的定律：
　情勢不妙，人人開溜。

▼Kohn 引申的莫非定律：
　禍不單行只是個開場。

▼McDonald 引申的莫非定律：
　不管處於何種情況，正確的行為方式要視後續
　情況而定。

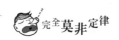

MURPHY'S LAW OF GOVERNMENT:

If anything can go wrong, it will do so in triplicate.

MAAHS' LAW:

Things go right so they can go wrong.

ADDENDUM TO MURPHY'S LAW:

In precise mathematical terms, $1 + 1 = 2$, where "=" is a symbol meaning "seldom if ever."

GUALTIERI'S LAW OF INERTIA:

Where there's a will, there's a won't.

MURPHY'S UNCERTAINTY PRINCIPLE:

You can know something has gone wrong only when you make an odd number of mistakes.

TUSSMAN'S LAW:

Nothing is as inevitable as a mistake whose time has come.

LAW OF PROBABLE DISPERSAL:

Whatever hits the fan will not be evenly distributed.

FAHNSTOCK'S RULE FOR FAILURE:

If at first you don't succeed, destroy all evidence that you tried.

EVANS' AND BJORN'S LAW:

No matter what goes wrong, there is always somebody who knew it would.

莫非的政府定律：

任何錯誤都是一式三份。

Maahs 的定律：

做對是為了出錯。

補充莫非定律：

就精確的數學而論，1＋1＝2，但其中「＝」這個符號意思是「偶而如此」。

Gualtieri 的慣性定律：

有志者事未必成。

莫非不確定原則：

只有犯了奇數個錯，你才會知道事情出錯了。

Tussman 的定律：

該來的錯誤，什麼也擋不住。

分散可能性定律：

注定要倒楣的時候，有些人會比別人更倒楣。（出自「shit hits the fan」指倒楣的事情發生了。）

Fahnstock 的失敗法則：

如果起步失利，別留下任何嘗試的痕跡。

Evan 和 Bjorn 的定律：

不管什麼出錯，總是有人早就料到。

 完全莫非定律

◣LANGSAM'S LAWS:

1. Everything depends.

2. Nothing is always.

3. Everything is something.

◣HELLRUNG'S LAW:

If you wait, it will go away.

◣Shavelson's Extension:

Having done its damage.

◣Grelb's Addition:

If it was bad, it'll be back.

◣GROSSMAN'S MISQUOTE OF H.L. MENCKEN:

Complex problems have simple, easy-to-understand wrong answers.

◣DUCHARME'S PRECEPT:

Opportunity always knocks at the least opportune moment.

◣FLUGG'S LAW:

When you need to knock on wood is when you realize the world is composed of aluminum and vinyl.

◣IMBESI'S LAW OF THE CONSERVATION OF FILTH:

In order for something to become clean, something else must become dirty.

◣Freeman's Extension:

But you can get everything dirty without getting anything clean.

◣FIRST POSTULATE OF ISO-MURPHISM:

Things equal to nothing else are equal to each other.

◤Langsam 的定律：
　1.一切視情況而定。
　2.沒有「永遠」這回事。
　3.沒有「必然」這回事。

◤Hellrung 的定律：
　你不變，局勢就變。

◤Shavelson 的引申：
　還留下一堆爛帳。

◤Grelb 的補充：
　如果好轉，還會再變壞。

◤Grossman 誤引 H.L. Mencken 的話：
　複雜的問題都有簡單易懂的錯誤答案。

◤Ducharme 的原理：
　機會總是來的不是時候。

◤Flugg 的定律：
　當你需要敲敲木頭去霉運時，才發現這世界是鋁跟塑膠做的。

◤Imbesi 的穢物不去定律：
　把一樣東西弄乾淨了，一定有另一樣變髒。

◤Freeman 的補充：
　不過什麼都弄髒，卻未必有別的會變乾淨。

◤規格莫非定律的第一個先決條件：
　與眾不同的東西，必然彼此雷同。

◥RUNE'S RULE:

If you don't care where you are, you ain't lost.

◥COIT-MURPHY'S STATEMENT ON THE POWER OF NEGATIVE THINKING:

It is impossible for an optimist to be pleasantly surprised.

◥FERGUSON'S PRECEPT:

A crisis is when you can't say, "Let's forget the whole thing."

◥THE UNAPPLICABLE LAW:

Washing your car to make it rain doesn't work.

◥MURPHY'S SAVING GRACE:

The worst is enemy of the bad.

◥THE CARDINAL CONUNDRUM:

An optimist believes we live in the best of all possible worlds. A pessimist fears this is true.

▼Rune 的法則：
不在乎在哪，就不算迷路。

▼莫非論悲觀想法的力量：
樂觀者無喜可驚。

▼Ferguson 的教訓：
所謂難關，就是連「乾脆忘掉這一切算了」都不能說。

▼不能用的定律：
洗車好讓老天爺下雨這招，是不會奏效的。

▼莫非的救命仙丹：
壞不敵更壞。

▼首要之謎：
樂觀者相信，再也沒有別的世界比我們所住的
世界更好。悲觀者害怕真的是如此。

NAESER'S LAW:

You can make it foolproof, but you can't make it damnfoolproof.

DUDE'S LAW DUALITY:

Of two possible events, only the undesired one will occur.

HANE'S LAW:

There is no limit to how bad things can get.

PERRUSSEL'S LAW:

There is no job so simple that it cannot be done wrong.

MAE WEST'S OBSERVATION:

To err is human, but it feels divine.

THINE'S LAW:

Nature abhors people.

BORKOWSKI'S LAW:

You can't guard against the arbitrary.

LACKLAND'S LAWS:

1. Never be first.
2. Never be last.
3. Never volunteer for anything.

HIGDON'S LAW:

Good judgment comes from bad experience.
Experience comes from bad judgment.

THE PAROUZZI PRINCIPLE:

Given a bad start, trouble will increase at an exponential rate.

▼ Naeser 的定律：

笨蛋可防，不過防不了大笨蛋。

▼ Dude 的二選一定律：

如果有兩個可能，只有不想要的那個會發生。

▼ Hane 的定律：

糟糕沒有限度。

▼ Perrussel 的定律：

再簡單的工作都會出錯。

▼ Mae West 的觀察：

錯屬人為，卻彷彿天意。

▼ Thine 的定律：

造化恨人。

▼ Borkowski 的定律：

意外無法可防。

▼ Lackland 的定律：

1.別搶先。

2.別殿後。

3.別自告奮勇。

▼ Higdon 的定律：

好判斷力來自壞經驗。

經驗來自壞判斷力。

▼ Parouzzi 的原則：

有個壞的開始，問題會以幾何級數增加。

◥THE CHI FACTOR:

Quantity = 1 / Quality; or, quantity is inversely proportional to quality.

◥LAW OF PARTICULATE ATTRACTION:

A flying particle will seek the nearest eye.

◥MESKIMEN'S LAW:

There's never time to do it right, but there's always time to do it over.

◥SCHOPENHAUER'S LAW OF ENTROPY:

If you put a spoonful of wine in a barrel full of sewage, you get sewage.

If you put a spoonful of sewage in a barrel full of wine, you get sewage.

◥ALLEN'S LAW:

Almost anything is easier to get into than to get out of.

▼Chi 變數：
　量＝1／質；也就是說，質與量成反比。

▼微塵吸引定律：
　飄動的灰塵總是就近找個眼睛沾上。

▼Meskimen 的定律：
　事情總是沒時間做好，卻總有時間重做。

▼Schopenhauer 的熵定律：
　把一匙酒加到一桶餿水裡，得到的是餿水。
　把一匙餿水加到一桶酒裡，得到的還是餿水。

▼Allen 的定律：
　事情幾乎都是起頭容易結束難。

FROTHINGHAM'S LAW:

Urgency varies inversely with importance.

THE ROCKEFELLER PRINCIPLE:

Never do anything you wouldn't be caught dead doing.

YOUNG'S LAW OF INANIMATE MOBILITY:

All inanimate objects can move just enough to get in your way.

LAW OF THE PERVERSITY OF NATURE:

You cannot successfully determine beforehand which side of the bread to butter.

LAW OF SELECTIVE GRAVITY:

An object will fall so as to do the most damage.

Jenning's Corollary:

The chance of the bread falling with the buttered side down is directly proportional to the cost of the carpet.

Klipstein's Corollary:

The most delicate component will be the one to drop.

SPRINKEL'S LAW:

Things always fall at right angles.

FULTON'S LAW OF GRAVITY:

The effort to catch a falling, breakable object will produce more destruction than if the object had been allowed to fall in the first place.

PAUL'S LAW:

You can't fall off the floor.

◤Frothingham 的定律：
緊急程度與重要性成反比。

◤Rockefeller 原則：
不會被逮個正著的事就不要做。

◤Young 的非生物移動定律：
所有無生命的物體，都會移動到正好礙著人的地方。

◤大自然的怪癖定律：
你沒辦法下定決心在麵包哪一面塗奶油。

◤選擇性地心引力定律：
東西不掉落則已，要不就會用破壞最大的方式掉落。

◤Jenning 的同理可證：
麵包落地時，塗奶油那一面著地的機率，與地毯的價格成正比。

◤Klipstein 的同理可證：
掉落的一定是最脆弱的東西。

◤Sprinkel 的定律：
東西總是垂直掉落。

◤Fulton 的重力定律：
想救掉落的易碎物，只會帶來更多破壞，不如讓它掉落算了。

◤Paul 的定律：
落到地板就無處可掉了。

PROBLEMATICS
問題學

SMITH'S LAW:

No real problem has a solution.

HOARE'S LAW OF LARGE PROBLEMS:

In side every large problem is a small problem struggling to get out.

THE SCHAINKER CONVERSE TO HOARE'S LAW OF LARGE PROBLEMS:

Inside every small problem is a larger problem struggling to get out.

BIG AL'S LAW:

A good solution can be successfully applied to almost any problem.

PEER'S LAW:

The solution to a problem changes the nature of the problem.

BARUCH'S OBSERVATION:

If all you have is a hammer, everything looks like a nail.

DISRAELI'S DICTUM:

Error is often more earnest than truth.

FOX ON PROBLEMATICS:

When a problem goes away, the people working to solve it do not.

WALDROP'S PRINCIPLE:

The person not here is the one working on the problem.

◥Smith 的定律：

　真正的問題無一可解。

◥Hoare 的大問題定律：

　每個大問題的肚子裡，都有個小問題拼命往外鑽。

◥Schainker 反用 Hoare 的大問題定律：

　每個小問題的肚子裡，都有個大問題拼命往外鑽。

◥Big Al 的定律：

　好辦法大概用到什麼問題上都管用。

◥Peer 的定律：

　解決問題的辦法會改變問題的性質。

◥Baruch 的觀察：

　如果你有一把槌子，看什麼都像釘子。

◥Disraeli 的格言：

　錯誤通常比真理還懇切。

◥Fox 看問題學：

　問題走了，解決問題的人卻賴著不走。

◥Waldrop 的原則：

　處理問題的人正是沒來的那個人。

◥Corollary:

If the person is not expected back, he is the one responsible for the problem.

◥BIONDI'S LAW:

If your project doesn't work, look for the part you didn't think was important.

◥VAN GOGH'S LAW:

Whatever plan one makes, there is a hidden difficulty somewhere.

◥THE ROMAN RULE:

The one who says it cannot be done should never interrupt the one who is doing it.

◥LAW OF THE GREAT IDEA:

The one time you come up with a great solution, somebody else has just solved the problem.

◥BLAIR'S OBSERVATION:

The best laid plans of mice and men are usually about equal.

◥SEAY'S LAW:

Nothing ever comes out as planned.

◥RUCKERT'S LAW:

There is nothing so small that it can't be blown out of proportion.

◥VAN HERPEN'S LAW:

The solving of a problem lies in finding the solvers.

◥同理可證：
如果這個人肯定不回來了，問題一定是由他負責。

◥Biondi 的定律：
如果計畫不奏效，看看你原本覺得無關緊要的部分。

◥梵谷的定律：
不管做什麼打算，總是有個難題等著你。

◥羅馬人的法則：
說某事絕對做不到的人，就不該打擾正在做這件事的人。

◥好主意定律：
你才想到妙法子，就有人正好把問題解決了。

◥Blair 的觀察：
對待老鼠和對待人類的絕佳方案通常差不了多少。

◥Seay 的定律：
事無不與願違。

◥Ruckert 的定律：
再小的事情都能鬧大。

◥Van Herpen 的定律：
解鈴只須繫鈴人。

HALL'S LAW:

The means justify the means. The approach to a problem is more important than its solution.

BAXTER'S LAW:

An error in the premise will appear in the conclusion.

McGEE'S FIRST LAW:

It's amazing how long it takes to complete something you are not working on.

▼Hall 的定律：
　手段就是目的。問題只問處理了沒，不問解決了沒。

▼Baxter 的定律：
　前提裡的錯誤會在結論裡出現。

▼McGee 的第一定律：
　沒花工夫的事情想收尾竟然要花那麼多時間，真教人詫異。

BUREAUCRATICS
官僚學

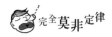

THE BUREAUCRACY PRINCIPLE:

Only a bureaucracy can fight a bureaucracy.

FOX ON BUREAUCRACY:

A bureaucracy can outwait anything.

Corollary:

Never get caught between two bureaucracies.

YOUNG'S LAW:

It is the dead wood that holds up the tree.

Corollary:

Just because it is still standing doesn't mean it is not dead.

HOFFSTEDT'S EMPLOYMENT PRINCIPLE:

Confusion creates jobs.

SOPER'S LAW:

Any bureaucracy reorganized to enhance efficiency is immediately indistinguishable from its predecessor.

GIOIA'S THEORY:

The person with the least expertise has the most opinions.

OWEN'S THEORY OF ORGANIZATIONAL DEVIANCE:

Every organization has an allotted number of positions to be filled by misfits.

Corollary:

Once a misfit leaves, another will be recruited.

◥官僚原則：
只有官僚才對付得了官僚。

◥Fox 看官僚：
官僚最能等。

◥以此類推：
千萬別夾在兩群官僚中間。

◥Young 的定律：
樹是靠死木構成的樹幹支撐。

◥以此類推：
還沒倒不見得就沒死。

◥Hoffstedt 的應用原則：
渾水才有魚摸。

◥Soper 的定律：
官僚系統若為了增加效率才改組，改組後立刻恢復原狀。

◥Gioia 的理論：
學識最淺的人意見最多（半桶水響叮噹）。

◥Owen 的組織變異理論：
每個組織總有些職位留給不稱職的人。

◥同理可證：
不稱職的人一走，立刻會有另一個不稱職的人
補上。

◥POST'S MANAGERIAL OBSERVATION:

The inefficiency and stupidity of the staff corresponds to the inefficiency and stupidity of the management.

◥AIGNER'S AXIOM:

No matter how well you perform your job, a superior will seek to modify the results.

◥THE PITFALLS OF GENIUS:

No boss will keep an employee who is right all the time.

◥MOLLISON'S BUREAUCRACY HYPOTHESIS:

If an idea can survive a bureaucratic review and be implemented, it wasn't worth doing.

◥PARKINSON'S FIFTH LAW:

If there is a way to delay an important decision, the good bureaucracy, public or private, will find it.

◥PARKINSON'S LAW OF DELAY:

Delay is the deadliest form of denial.

◥LOFTUS' THEORY ON PERSONNEL RECRUITMENT:

1. Faraway talent always seems better than home-developed talent.
2. Personnel recruiting is a triumph of hope over experience.

◥LOFTUS' LAW OF MANAGEMENT:

Some people manage by the book, even though they don't know who wrote the book or even what the book is.

▼Post 看管理：

幕僚的沒效率與愚行，正反映了管理階層的沒效率與愚行。

▼Aigner 的格言：

你做得再好，上司總是會想辦法挑毛病。

▼天才的危機：

世上沒有老闆容得下永遠正確的手下。

▼Mollison 對官僚的假設：

任何想法若能通過官僚審核又能付諸實行，一定不值得做。

▼Parkinson 的第五定律：

重要決策只要能拖延，不管公家或民間，高竿的官僚一定有辦法拖延。

▼Parkinson 的延遲定律：

延遲是最要命的拒絕。

▼Loftus 的人事招募理論：

1. 遠來和尚會唸經。
2. 招募新人表示希望勝過經驗。

▼Loftus 的管理定律：

有些人照書本所教來管理，即使他搞不清楚書是誰寫的，或者是在討論什麼。

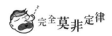

JOE'S LAW:

The inside contact that you have developed at great expense is the first person to be let go in any reorganization.

THE LIPPMAN DILEMMA:

People specialize in their area of greatest weakness.

THINGS THAT CAN BE COUNTED ON IN A CRISIS:

MARKETING says yes.

FINANCE says no.

LEGAL has to review it.

PERSONNEL is concerned.

PLANNING is frantic.

ENGINEERING is above it all.

MANUFACTURING wants more floor space.

TOP MANAGEMENT wants someone responsible.

COHN'S LAW:

In any bureaucracy, paperwork increases as you spend more and more time reporting on the less and less you are doing. Stability is achieved when you spend all of your time reporting on the nothing you are doing.

SWEENEY'S LAW:

The length of a progress report is inversely proportional to the amount of progress.

MORRIS' LAW OF CONFERENCES:

The most interesting paper will be scheduled simultaneously with the second most interesting paper.

Joe 的定律：

你花了好多工夫才安插的耳目，在組織更動時卻是第一個得放走的人。

Lippman 的兩難：

人總是專精自己最弱的一環。

困境中必然的現象：

行銷說行。

財務說不行。

法務一定得查核。

人事表達關切。

企劃亂了陣腳。

工程主掌一切。

生產需要更多樓面。

最高當局希望有人扛責任。

Cohn 的定律：

任何官僚系統都會用愈來愈多的書面資料，呈報愈來愈少的績效。穩定狀態是把所有的時間花在報告各單位什麼事也沒做。

Sweeney 的定律：

進度報告的長度與進度成反比。

Morris 的會議定律：

最引人興趣的兩篇報告，一定排在同一時間進行。

COLLINS' CONFERENCE PRINCIPLE:

The speaker with the most monotonous voice speaks after the big meal.

McNAUGHTON'S RULE:

Any argument worth making within the bureaucracy must be capable of being expressed in a simple declarative sentence that is obviously true once stated.

PATTON'S LAW:

A good plan today is better than a perfect plan tomorrow.

JACOBSON'S LAW:

The less work an organization produces, the more frequently it reorganizes.

◥Collin 的會議原則：

大餐後的致詞人，語調最呆板。

◥McNaughton 的法則：

值得在官僚體系內進行的討論，一定可以用一句話簡單明白地表達，而且一聽就知道不用說也知道。

◥Patton 的定律：

今天的好計劃，勝過明日的完美計劃。

◥Jacobson 的定律：

組織的產出愈少，重組的次數就愈多。

HIERARCHIOLOGY
階級學

PERKINS' POSTULATE:

The bigger they are, the harder they hit.

HARRISON'S POSTULATE:

For every action, there is an equal and opposite criticism.

ROGERS' RULE:

Authorization for a project will be granted only when none of the authorizers can be blamed if the project fails but when all of the authorizers can claim credit if it succeeds.

GATES' LAW:

The only important information in a hierarchy is who knows what.

RULE OF DEFACTUALIZATION:

Information deteriorates upward through bureaucracies.

BACHMAN'S INEVITABILITY THEOREM:

The greater the cost of putting a plan into operation, the less chance there is of abandoning the plan—even if it subsequently becomes irrelevant.

Corollary:

The higher the level of prestige accorded to the people behind the plan, the less chance there is of abandoning it.

CONWAY'S LAW:

In any organization there will always be one person who knows what is going on. This person must be fired.

Perkin 的假設：

人爬得愈高，打擊愈嚴重。（變化自 "The harder they come, the harder they fall." 爬得愈高，跌得愈重。）

Harrison 的假設：

任何作為總有等量的負面批評。

Rogers 的法則：

方案要符合下列條件才可能通過：如果方案失敗，批准的人都不必負責；要是事成，批准的人都可以邀功。

Gates 的定律：

階級體系裡首先要知道的是誰掌握了什麼訊息。

說空話法則：

話愈往高層傳愈走樣。

Bachman 的不可避免理論：

計劃付諸實行的成本愈高，放棄的機會就愈少——就算該計劃後來變得不值得做。

同理可證：

計劃背後的主事者地位愈高，放棄的機會就愈少。

Conway 的定律：

不管哪個單位，總會有人知道內幕消息。這個人留不得。

FOX ON LEVELOLOGY:

What will get you promoted on one level will get you killed on another.

STEWART'S LAW OF RETROACTION:

It is easier to get forgiveness than permission.

FIRST RULE OF SUPERIOR INFERIORITY:

Don't let your superiors know you're better than they are.

WHISTLER'S LAW:

You never know who's right, but you always know who's in charge.

SPENCER'S LAWS OF DATA:

1. Anyone can make a decision given enough facts.

2. A good manager can make a decision without enough facts.

3. A perfect manager can operate in perfect ignorance.

GOTTLIEB'S RULE:

The boss who attempts to impress employees with his or her knowledge of intricate details has lost sight of the final objective.

DINGLE'S LAW:

When somebody drops something, everybody will kick it around instead of picking it up.

KUSHNER'S LAW:

The chances of anybody doing anything are inversely proportional to the number of other people who are in a position to do it instead.

PFEIFER'S PRINCIPLE:

Never make a decision you can get someone else to make.

Fox 看層次學：
在某個階段可擢升的功績，到了另一個階段就是身敗名裂的禍因。

Stewart 的追溯定律：
求原諒易，求批准難。

高位低能的第一法則：
別讓上頭的人知道你比他們行。

Whistler 的定律：
你從不知道誰對，但你一定清楚誰是老大。

Spencer 的資料庫定律：
1. 只要有資料，誰都能做決策。
2. 高明的管理者不必足夠的資料也能做決策。
3. 完美的管理者，什麼都不知道也一樣能幹。

Gottlieb 的法則：
想讓手下以為自己知道的事鉅細靡遺的老闆，已經看不到最終目標。

Dingle 的定律：
東西掉地上，大家只會踢開，沒人會撿起來。

Kushner 的定律：
有事可忙的機會，與可以代替做這件事的人數成反比。

Pfeifer 的原則：
決策能找人做就別自己做。

Corollary:

No one keeps a record of decisions you could have made but didn't. Everyone keeps a record of your bad ones.

THAL'S LAW:

For every vision, there is an equal and opposite revision.

MacDONALD'S LAW:

It's tough to get reallocated when you're the one who's redundant.

WELLINGTON'S LAW OF COMMAND:

The cream rises to the top.

So does the scum.

HELLER'S LAW:

The first myth of management is that it exists.

Johnson's Corollary:

Nobody really knows what is going on anywhere within the organization.

THE PETER PRINCIPLE:

In a hierarchy, every employee tends to rise to his level of incompetence.

Corollaries:

1. In time, every post tends to be occupied by an employee who is incompetent to carry out his or her duties.
2. Work is accomplished by those employees who have not yet reached their level of incompetence.

▼同理可證：

　　沒人會記得你能做而未做的決策。但做錯決策，卻誰也不會忘。

▼Thal 的定律：

　　有遠見就有同等份量的相反修正。

▼MacDonald 的定律：

　　冗員想調動，可謂難上加難。

▼Wellington 指揮權定律：

　　奶油浮到上層。

　　無用的浮渣也會。

▼Heller 的定律：

　　關於管理的最大迷思，是以爲眞有管理這回事。

▼Johnson's 同理可證：

　　組織情況如何，內部上下無人清楚。

▼彼得定律：

　　人爬得到的最高位階，往往就是他無法勝任的職位。

▼同理可證：

　　1. 總有一天，所有工作都會由不適任的人擔任。

　　2. 那些還沒升到不能勝任的地位的人，才是眞正在做事的人。

 完全莫非定律

PETER'S INVERSION:

Internal consistency is valued more highly than efficiency service.

PETER'S HIDDEN POSTULATE ACCORDING TO GODIN:

Every employee begins at his level of competence.

PETER'S OBSERVATION:

Super-competence is more objectionable than incompetence.

PETER'S LAW OF EVOLUTION:

Competence always contains the seed of incompetence.

PETER'S RULE FOR CREATIVE INCOMPETENCE:

Create the impression that you have already reached your level of incompetence.

PETER'S THEOREM:

Incompetence plus incompetence equals incompetence.

PETER'S LAW OF SUBSTITUTION:

Look after the molehills and the mountains will look after themselves.

PETER'S PROGNOSIS:

Spend sufficient time in confirming the need and the need will disappear.

PETER'S PLACEBO:

An ounce of image is worth a pound of performance.

GODIN'S LAW:

Generalizedness of incompetence is directly proportional to highestness in hierarchy.

▼彼得反律：
　內部的一致比工作效率更受重視。

▼Godin 找出彼得定律的隱含原則：
　員工都從自己能力所及的地方起步。

▼Peter 的觀察：
　能力過人所受的阻力比無能更大。

▼Peter 的進化定律：
　能力永遠包含無能的種子。

▼Peter 有創意的無能法則：
　不妨製造已到達無能地步的假象。

▼Peter 的定理：
　無能加無能等於無能。

▼Peter 的替代定律：
　小題大作，大題自然就小作。（出自 "make a moution out of a molehill" 意指小題大作）

▼Peter 的預測：
　花足夠的時間確定某個需求，這個需求就會消失。

▼Peter 的安慰劑：
　一盎斯的形象等於一磅的功績。

▼Godin 的定律：
　無能的分佈廣度與階級的高度成正比。

◥FREEMAN'S RULE:

Circumstances can force a generalized incompetent to become competent, at least in a specialized field.

◥VAIL'S AXIOM:

In any human enterprise, work seeks the lowest hierarchical level.

◥IMHOFF'S LAW:

The organization of any bureaucracy is very much like a septic tank—the really big chunks always rise to the top.

◥PARKINSON'S AXIOMS:

1. An official wants to multiply subordinates, not rivals.
2. Officials make work for each other.

▼Freeman 的法則：
環境可使普遍的無能變爲能幹，至少專業領域是如此。

▼Vail 的格言：
在人類的組織裡，工作都落在最低階級身上。

▼Imhoff 的定律：
任何官僚組織都酷似化糞池——大塊的總是浮到上頭來。

▼Parkinson 的格言：
　1.當官的想增加的是手下，不是對手。
　2.官官相助。

SOCIOLOGY'S IRON LAW OF OLIGARCHY:

In every organized activity, no matter what the sphere, a small number will become the oligarchical leaders and the others will follow.

OESER'S LAW:

There is a tendency for the person in the most powerful position in an organization to spend all of his or her time serving on committees and signing letters.

ZYMURGY'S LAW OF VOLUNTEER LABOR:

People are always available for work in the past tense.

THE SALARY AXIOM:

The pay raise is just large enough to increase your taxes and just small enough to have no effect on your take-home pay.

MURPHY'S OBSERVATION ON BUSINESS:

The toughest thing in business is minding your own.

LAW OF COMMUNICATIONS:

The inevitable result of improved and enlarged communication between different levels in a hierarchy is a vastly increased area of misunderstanding.

DOW'S LAW:

In a hierarchical organization, the higher the level, the greater the confusion.

BUNUEL'S LAW:

Overdoing things is harmful in all cases, even when it comes to efficiency.

▼社會學裡寡頭政治的鐵律：

在任何有組織的活動裡，不管哪種環境，一小撮人會成為領導中心，其餘的人會跟著走。

▼Oeser 的定律：

情況往往如此：組織裡權力最大的人物，把時間全花在主持各個委員會與信件簽名上頭。

▼Zymurgy 的自願勞動定律：

人們有空工作的時間總是過去式。

▼薪水的箴言：

加薪的幅度正好大到足以增加稅金，可是卻又沒有大到能有多餘的錢拿回家。

▼莫非看企業：

工作裡最難的莫過於別管閒事。

▼溝通定律：

階級組織裡各個層次若試圖改善並增加溝通管道，必然的結果就是誤解的層面也會大幅增加。

▼Dow 的定律：

層層管制的組織裡，階級愈高愈混亂。

▼Bunuel 的定律：

事情過火總是不好，所以效率也不該太高。

◥SPARK'S TEN RULES FOR THE PROJECT MANAGER:

1. Strive to look tremendously important.

2. Attempt to be seen with important people.

3. Speak with authority; however, only expound on the obvious and proven facts.

4. Don't engage in arguments, but if cornered, ask an irrelevant question and lean back with a satisfied grin while your opponent tries to figure out what'S going on—then quickly change the subject.

5. Listen intently while others are arguing the problem. Pounce on a trite statement and bury them with it.

6. If a subordinate asks you a pertinent question, look at him as if he has lost his sense. When he looks down, paraphrase the question back at him.

7. Obtain a brilliant assignment, but keep out of sight and out of the limelight.

8. Walk at a fast pace when out of the office—this keeps questions from subordinates and superiors at a minimum.

9. Always keep the office door closed. This puts visitors on the defensive and also makes it look as if you are always in an important conference.

10. Give all orders verbally. Never write anything down that might go into a "Watergate."

◥TRUTHS OF MANAGEMENT:

1. Think before you act; it's not your money.

2. All good management is the expression of one great idea.

3. No executive devotes effort to proving himself wrong.

4. If sophisticated calculations are needed to justify an action, don't do it.

Spark 給企劃經理的十條法則：

1. 拼命讓自己顯得重要無比。

2. 想辦法跟重要人物同時出現。

3. 想辦法跟當權者說話；不過，只解釋那些顯而易見、已經證實的事。

4. 別加入爭論，如果牽扯進去了，就問些不相干的問題，堆出滿足的笑容往後一靠，讓對方搞不清楚所以然——這時候趕快換話題。

5. 別人在爭論問題的時候先仔細聽。然後用老生常談，把那些傢伙殺個措手不及。

6. 如果屬下問了一個切題的問題，先瞪著他讓他覺得自己失言。等他垂頭喪氣，再用這個問題反問他。

7. 爭取好的任務，不過別讓人看見，也別引起注意。

8. 一出辦公室就快步走——這樣可以讓屬下與上司沒機會問問題。

9. 辦公室的門最好都關著。這樣讓來訪者有所顧忌，也讓人家覺得你總是有個重要會議在開。

10. 命令全以口頭傳達，千萬不要留下書面證據，以免成為水門案的證據。

管理的真理：

1. 三思而後行，錢可不是你的。

2. 所有好的管理都表達了同一個偉大的想法。

3. 沒有管理人會花時間來證明自己錯了。

4. 如果行動需要費盡心思來辯解就別做。

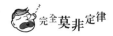

◤JAY'S LAW OF LEADERSHIP:

Changing things is central to leadership, and changing them before anyone else is creativeness.

◤MATCH'S MAXIM:

A fool in a high station is like a man on the top of a high mountain; everything appears small to him and he appears small to everybody.

◤WORKER'S DILEMMA:

1. No matter how much you do, you'll never do enough.
2. What you don't do is always more important than what you do do.

◤IRON LAW OF DISTRIBUTION:

Them that has, gets.

◤THE ARMY AXIOM:

Any order that can be misunderstood has been misunderstood.

◤LAW OF SOCIO-ECONOMICS:

In a hierarchical system, the rate of pay for a given task increases in inverse ratio to the unpleasantness and difficulty of the task.

◤PUTT'S LAW:

Technology is dominated by two types of people:
Those who understand what they do not manage.
Those who manage what they do not understand.

◤JONES' LAW:

The man who can smile when things go wrong has thought of someone he can blame it on.

▼Jay 的領導定律：
改變是領導方法的中心要旨，搶在大家之前改變則是創意。

▼Match 的格言：
居於高位的傻瓜就像站在高峰上的人；他看別人都覺得人家藐
小，別人看他也覺得他藐小。

▼勞工的難題：
1. 不管做多少，總是不夠。
2. 沒做到的，總是比做了的重要。

▼分配的鐵律：
富者愈富。

▼軍隊的箴言：
有可能誤解的命令全都被誤解了。

▼社會經濟定律：
在層級分明的體系裡，任何的報酬與任務的煩度及難度成反比。

▼Putt 的定律：
科技被兩種人霸佔：
一種是懂自己不管的。
一種是管自己不懂的。

▼Jones 的定律：
事情出錯還笑得出來的人，心裡已經想到代罪
羔羊。

COMMITTEEOLOGY
委員會學

McKERNAN'S MAXIM:

Those who are unable to learn from past meetings are condemned to repeat them.

COURTOIS' RULE:

If people listened to themselves more often, they would talk less.

OLD AND KAHN'S LAW:

The efficiency of a committee meeting is inversely proportional to the number of participants and the time spent on deliberations.

SHANAHAN'S LAW:

The length of a meeting rises with the square of the number of people present.

LAW OF TRIVIALITY:

The time spent on any item of the agenda will be in inverse proportion to the sum involved.

ISSAWI'S LAWS OF COMMITTO-DYNAMICS:

1. *Comitas comitatum, omnia comitas.*
2. The less you enjoy serving on committees, the more likely you will be pressed to do so.

MATILDA'S LAW OF SUB-COMMITTEE FORMATION:

If you leave the room, you're elected.

THIRD LAW OF COMMITTO-DYNAMICS:

Those most opposed to serving on committees are made chairpersons.

▼McKernan 的格言：
　　不能從開過的會議學到教訓，就註定要重開那些會。

▼Courtois 的法則：
　　多聽自己講什麼話，就會少說些話。

▼Old 和 Kahn 的定律：
　　委員會開會的效率，與出席人數及討論時間成反比。

▼Shanahan 的定律：
　　會議的長度以出席人數的平方比增加。

▼瑣事定律：
　　程序表上各事項所花的時間，與涉及的經費成反比。

▼Issawi 的委員會動力學：
　　1. *Comitas comitatum, omnia comitas.*
　　2. 你愈不喜歡主持開會事務，你就愈可能受推派管這檔事。

▼Matilda 的次級委員會形成定律：
　　離開會場的人就會當選。

▼委員會動力學第三定律：
　　最不愛主持會務者，就會當選主席。

MITCHELL'S LAWS OF COMMITTEEOLOGY:

1. Any simple problem can be made insoluble if enough conferences are held to discuss it.
2. Once the way to screw up a project is presented for consideration it will invariably be accepted as the soundest solution.
3. After the solution screws up the project, all those who initially endorsed it will say, " wish I had voiced my reservations at the time."

KIM'S RULE OF COMMITTEES:

If an hour has been spent amending a sentence, someone will move to delete the paragraph.

THE ELEVENTH COMMANDMENT:

Thou shalt not committee.

KENNEDY'S COMMENT ON COMMITTEES:

A committee is twelve people doing the work of one.

KIRBY'S COMMENT ON COMMITTEES:

A committee is the only life form with twelve stomachs and no brain.

HENDRICKSON'S LAW:

If a problem causes many meetings, the meetings eventually become more important than the problem.

LORD FALKLAND'S RULE:

When it is not necessary to make a decision, it is necessary not to make a decision.

▼Mitchell 的委員會學定律：

1. 問題再簡單，只要開夠多次會來討論，都可以變得無法解決。
2. 把計畫搞砸的方法一旦提出來供人參考，最後無一不被大家推舉為最可靠的解決辦法。
3. 等計畫給那個解決辦法搞砸了，所有當初為那個方法背書的人都說，「我當時真該把心中的疑慮說出來。」

▼Kim 的委員會法則：

如果修飾一句話花了一個鐘頭，就會有人動議把整段刪掉。

▼第十一誡：

不准成立委員會。

▼Kennedy 評委員會：

所謂委員會是十二個人做一個人做的事。

▼Kirby 評委員會：

只有委員會這種怪胎有十二個胃卻沒有腦袋。

▼Hendrickson 的定律：

如果問題造成許多會議，這些會議最後會比問題本身重要。

▼Lord Falkland 的法則：

沒必要做決定，就有必要不做決定。

FAIRFAX'S LAW:

Any facts which, when included in the argument, give the desired results, are fair facts for the argument.

HUTCHINS' LAW:

You can't outtalk a man who knows what he's talking about.

FAHNSTOCK'S LAW OF DEBATE:

Any issue worth debating is worth avoiding altogether.

HARTZ'S LAW OF RHETORIC:

Any argument carried far enough will end up in semantics.

GOURD'S AXIOM:

A meeting is an event at which the minutes are kept and the hours are lost.

FIRST LAW OF BUSINESS MEETINGS:

The lead in a pencil will break in direct proportion to the importance of the notes being taken.

▼Fairfax 的定律：

　　爭論中可以促成結論的事實，正是挑起爭端的事實。

▼Hutchins 的定律：

　　你說不過知道自己在說什麼的人。

▼Fahnstock 的爭論定律：

　　任何值得爭論的話題，都值得避而不談。

▼Hartz 的修辭定律：

　　爭論到最後都不過是語意的爭辯。

▼Gourd 的箴言：

　　開會這種事，省下幾分鐘卻浪費數小時。

▼商業會議第一定律：

　　筆心斷裂的機率與筆下要點的重要性成正比。

◥SECOND LAW OF BUSINESS MEETINGS:

If there are two possible ways to spell a person's name, you will pick the wrong spelling.

◥TRUMAN'S LAW:

If you cannot convince them, confuse them.

◥FIRST LAW OF DEBATE:

Never argue with a fool—people might not know the difference.

◥SWIPPLE'S RULE OF ORDER:

He who shouts loudest has the floor.

◥RAYBURN'S RULE:

If you want to get along, go along.

◥BOREN'S LAWS:

1. When in doubt, mumble.
2. When in trouble, delegate.
3. When in charge, ponder.

◥PARKER'S RULE OF PARLIAMENTARY PROCEDURE:

A motion to adjourn is always in order.

▼商業會議第二定律：
如果某人的名字有兩種拼法，你選的一定是錯的。

▼Truman 的定律：
說服不了別人，就把他們搞糊塗。

▼爭論第一原則：
別跟傻子爭論──旁人會以為你們是同類。

▼Swipple 的命令法則：
大聲的人就有理。

▼Rayburn 的法則：
想吃得開就別頂嘴。

▼Boren 的定律：
1. 不清楚就含糊其詞。
2. 有困難就派給別人。
3. 責任在身就三思而後行。

▼Parker 的國會程序法則：
休會的動議總是進行順利。

STATESMANSHIP AND ECONOMURPHOLOGY

政壇與經濟專家莫非學

LIEBERMAN'S LAW:

Everybody lies, but it doesn't matter since nobody listens.

LAW OF THE LIE:

No matter how often a lie is shown to be false, there will remain a percentage of people who believe it true.

THE SAUSAGE PRINCIPLE:

People who love sausage and respect the law should never watch either one being made.

JACQUIN'S POSTULATE ON DEMOCRATIC GOVERNMENT:

No person's life, liberty or property are safe while the legislature is in session.

TODD'S TWO POLITICAL PRINCIPLES:

1. No matter what they're telling you, they're not telling you the whole truth.
2. No matter what they're talking about, they're talking about money.

ANDRA'S POLITICAL POSTULATE:

Foundation of a party signals the dissolution of the movement.

KAMIN'S LAW:

When attempting to predict and forecast macro-economic moves of economic legislation by a politician, never be misled by what he says; instea—watch what he does.

THE WATERGATE PRINCIPLE:

Government corruption is always reported in the past tense.

Lieberman 的定律：

大家都說謊，不過無妨，反正沒人聽。

謊話定律：

不管謊話被揭穿多少次，總是有固定百分比的人信以為真。

香腸原則：

愛吃香腸及尊重法律的人，絕對不要去看這兩種東西的製造過程。

Jacquin 的民主政治前提：

國會立法期間，任何人的身家財產與自由都不安全。

Todd 的兩條政治原則：

1. 不管別人跟你說了什麼，其中必定有所保留。
2. 不管談的是什麼話題，談的都是錢。

Andra 的政治感想：

政黨的成立表示該政治運動已告瓦解。

Kamin 的定律：

政客擬定經濟法案時，若要預測其中總體經濟動向，千萬別給他的話騙了——要看他的作為。

水門案原則：

政府的腐敗都是以過去式報導。

ALINSKY'S RULE FOR RADICALS:

Those who are most moral are farthest from the problem.

MARX'S RULE OF POLITICS:

As soon as they become rich, they become Republican.

RULE OF POLITICAL PROMISES:

Truth varies.

LEE'S LAW:

In any dealings with a collective body of people, the people will always be more tacky than originally expected.

EVAN'S LAW:

If you can keep your head when all about you are losing theirs, then you just don't understand the problem.

RUSK'S LAW OF DELEGATION:

Where an exaggerated emphasis is placed upon delegation, responsibility, like sediment, sinks to the bottom.

THE GUPPY LAW:

When outrageous expenditures are divided finely enough, the public will not have enough stake in any one expenditure to squelch it.

Corollary:

Enough guppies can eat a treasury.

WIKER'S LAW:

Government expands to absorb revenue and then some.

▼Alinsky 的偏激份子法則：
　最有道德的人離問題最遠。

▼Marx 的政治法則：
　人一有錢就加入共和黨。

▼政治承諾法則：
　真理會變。

▼Lee 的法則：
　跟一群各路人馬湊成的組織打交道，他們絕對比原先預料的難
　纏。

▼Evan 的法則：
　眾人皆醉而你還能獨醒，那就是你不了解問題。

▼Rusk 的指派定律：
　愈是煞有介事指派的工作，其權責就像沈澱物一樣沉得愈低。

▼熱帶魚法則：
　如果一筆離譜的支出項目分得夠細，每個項目關係到人民的利益
　都極少，就沒人會說話。

▼同理可證：
　只要魚夠多，可以把國庫吃光光。

▼Wiker 的定律：
　擴充政府以消耗歲入，接著就會有人跟進。

完全莫非定律

GOOD'S RULE FOR DEALING WITH BUREAUCRA-CIES:

When the government bureau's remedies do not match your problem, you modify the problem, not the remedy.

MARKS' LAW OF MONETARY EQUALIZATION:

A fool and your money are soon partners.

HEISENBERG PRINCIPLE OF INVESTMENT:

You may know where the market is going, but you can't possibly know where it's going after that.

JEFF'S THEORY OF THE STOCK MARKET:

The price of a stock moves inversely to the number of shares purchased.

HORNGREN'S OBSERVATION:

Among economists, the real world is often a special case.

HELGA'S RULE:

Say no, then negotiate.

GLYME'S FORMULA FOR SUCCESS:

The secret of success is sincerity. Once you can fake that you've got it made.

O'BRIEN'S LAW:

Nothing is ever done for the right reasons.

SPENCER'S LAWS OF ACCOUNTANCY:

1. Trial balances don't.
2. Working capital doesn't.
3. Liquidity tends to run out.
4. Return on investments won't.

Good 的對付官僚的法則：

要是政府當局的補救辦法不符合你的問題，該修正的是你的問題
而不是補救辦法。

Mark 的均富定律：

你的錢就是會與傻瓜合夥。

Heisenberg 投資原則：

你也許知道市場會走到哪，可是之後怎麼走你卻不可能知道。

Jeff 的股市理論：

股價的變動與買進的股數成反比。

Horngren 的觀察：

真實的世界給經濟學者一說都成了特例。

Helga 的法則：

先拒絕再妥協。

Glyme 的成功秘笈：

成功的秘訣是誠懇。只要你裝得出來就成功了。

O'Brien 的定律：

天下事從來不按牌理出牌。

Spencer 的會計定律：

1. 試算不平衡。
2. 營業資本不夠用。
3. 流動資本會用光。
4. 投資沒有回報。

PRICE'S LAWS:

1. If everybody doesn't want it, nobody gets it.

2. Mass man must be served by mass means.

3. Everything is contagious.

BROWN'S RULES OF LEADERSHIP:

1. To succeed in politics, it is often necessary to rise above your principles.

2. The best way to succeed in politics is to find a crowd that's going somewhere and get in front of them.

THE RULE OF LAW:

If the facts are against you, argue the law.

If the law is against you, argue the facts.

If the facts and the law are against you, yell like hell.

MILES' LAW:

Where you stand depends on where you sit.

▼價格定律：

　　1. 如果每個人都不想要，那誰也得不到。

　　2. 大而化之的人就以大而化之的方法對付。

　　3. 什麼都會傳染。

▼Brown 的領導法則：

　　1. 想在政壇上成功，常常得超越自己本來的原則。

　　2. 在政壇成功的最佳辦法，就是先找到朝某個方向移動的群眾，
　　　然後趕到他們前頭。

▼法律的法則：

　　證據對你不利，就在法律上爭取。

　　法律對你不利，就討論證據。

　　證據、法律都對你不利，就震天喊冤。

▼Miles 的定律：

　　你的地位全看你坐在哪個位置。

FIBLEY'S EXTENSION TO MILES' LAW:

Where you sit depends on who you know.

FOX ON POWER:

Arrogance is too often the companion of excellence.

WALTON'S LAW OF POLITICS:

A fool and his money are soon elected.

THE FIFTH RULE OF POLITICS:

When a politician gets an idea, he usually gets it wrong.

WILKIE'S LAW:

A good slogan can stop analysis for fifty years.

SHERMAN'S RULE OF PRESS CONFERENCES:

The explanation of a disaster will be made by a stand-in.

ROCHE'S LAW:

Every American crusade winds up as a racket.

MILLER'S LAW:

Exceptions prove the rule—and wreck the budget.

BUCKWALD'S LAW:

As the economy gets better, everything else gets worse.

OGDEN NASH'S LAW:

Progress may have been all right once, but it went on too long.

FINNIGAN'S LAW:

The farthey away the future is, the better it looks.

Fibley 補充 Miles 的定律：
你坐在哪個位置就看你的人脈。

Fox 論權力：
傲慢往往伴隨在優異左右。

Walton 的政治定律：
傻子有錢很快就當選。

第五政治法則：
政客有了想法，通常是錯的。

Wilkie 的定律：
一句好口號可以讓人停止分析五十年。

Sherman 的記者招待會法則：
大災難交由代言人解釋。

Roche 的定律：
美國人一動員，結果都是大拜拜。

Miller 的定律：
例外證實了法則——也搞垮了預算。

Buckwald 的定律：
經濟轉好，別的就全轉壞。

Ogden Nash 的定律：
進步起先還差強人意，只是進行太久了。

Finnigan 的定律：
愈遠的未來看來愈美好。

▼ SIMON'S LAW OF DESTINY:

Glory may be fleeting, but obscurity is forever.

▼ THOMPSON'S THEOREM:

When the going gets weird, the weird turn pro.

▼ McCLAUGHRY'S LAW OF ZONING:

Where zoning is not needed, it will work perfectly. Where it is desperately needed, it always breaks down.

▼ MURPHY'S MONETARY MAXIM:

Inflation is never having it so good and parting with it so fast.

▼ FIRST LAW OF POLITICS:

Stay in with the outs.

▼ PARKS' LAW OF INSURANCE RATES AND TAXES:

Whatever goes up, stays up.

▼ FIRST LAW OF MONEY DYNAMICS:

A surprise monetary windfall will be accompanied by an unexpected expense of the same amount.

▼ ROBBINS' MINI-MAX RULE OF GOVERNMENT:

Any minimum criteria set will be the maximum value used.

▼ LOWE'S LAW:

Success always occurs in private, and failure in full public view.

◤Simon 的命運定律：
　榮耀不常久，卑微千百年。

◤Thompson 的理論：
　情況變怪，怪人就變專家。

◤McClaughry 的分區定律：
　無需分區的地方，分區作業順利。急需分區的地方，一定分得一
　團糟。

◤莫非金錢格言：
　通貨膨脹就是美得空前，去得奇快。

◤政治的第一定律：
　拉攏在野黨。

◤Parks 的保險利率及稅賦定律：
　全都只漲不減。

◤金錢動力學定律第一條：
　意外之財總是跟隨著一筆同樣數目的意外支出。

◤Robbins 的政府高低限度法則：
　一切最低限度都用來當作最大值。

◤Lowe 的定律：
　成功往住人後發生，失敗卻眾目睽睽。

EXPERTSMANSHIP
專家經

HOROWITZ'S RULE:

Wisdom consists of knowing when to avoid perfection.

DE NEVERS' LAW OF COMPLEXITY:

The simplest subjects are the ones you don't know anything about.

CHRISTIE-DAVIES' THEOREM:

If your facts are wrong but your logic is perfect, then your conclusions are inevitable false. Therefore, by making mistakes in your logic, you have at least a random chance of coming to a correct conclusion.

McCLELLAN'S LAW OF COGNITION:

Only new categories escape the stereotyped thinking associated with old abstractions.

HARTZ'S UNCERTAINTY PRINCIP LE:

Ambiguity is invariant.

DE NEVERS' LAW OF DEBATE:

Two monologues do not make a dialogue.

EMERSON'S OBSERVATION:

In every work of genius we recognize our rejected thoughts.

HIRAM'S LAW:

If you consult enough experts you can confirm any opinion.

JORDAN'S LAW:

An informant who never produces misinformation is too deviant to be trusted.

DE NEVERS' LOST LAW:

Never speculate on that which can be known for certain.

◥Horowitz 的法則：
　智慧在於知道何時避免完美。

◥De Nevers 的複雜定律：
　一無所知的事最簡單。

◥Christie-Davies 的理論：
　如果事實錯誤而理論正確，結論必錯無疑。因此邏輯裡出了錯，
　至少可能碰運氣得到正確的結論。

◥McClellan 的構思定律：
　只有新事物才能擺脫舊理論背後的刻板想法。

◥Hartz 的不確定原則：
　模稜兩可是常數。

◥De Nevers 的爭論定律：
　各說各話並不算是對談。

◥Emerson 的觀察：
　天才所做的事情，都有我們棄而不用的想法。

◥Hiram 的定律：
　只要請教過夠多的專家，什麼看法都是對的。

◥Jordan 的定律：
　從來不給錯誤資料的資料提供者，簡直反常得
　不能信賴。

◥De Nevers 的失敗定律：
　千萬別在八九不離十的事情上投機。

LAS VEGAS LAW:

Never bet on a loser because you think his luck is bound to change.

VAN ROY'S FIRST LAW:

If you can distinguish between good advice and bad advice, then you don't need advice.

HOWE'S LAW:

Everyone has a scheme that will not work.

MUNDER'S COROLLARY TO HOWE'S LAW:

Everyone who does not work has a scheme that does.

FOX ON DECISIVENESS:

1. Decisiveness is not in itself a virtue.
2. To decide not do decide is a decision. To fail to decide is a failure.
3. An important reason for an executive's existence is to make sensible exceptions to policy.

RULE OF THE OPEN MIND:

People who are resistant to change cannot resist change for the worse.

ELY'S KEY TO SUCCESS:

Create a need and fill it.

BRALEK'S RULE FOR SUCCESS:

Trust only those who stand to lose as much as you when things go wrong.

拉斯維加斯定律：

千萬別以為輸家要轉運了，就把注押在他身上。

Van Roy 的第一定律：

如果分得清好建議與壞建議，就根本不需要建議。

Howe 的定律：

誰都有一套行不通的計策。

Munder 類推 Howe 的定律：

不做事的人總有個行得通的計策。

Fox 看果斷：

1. 果斷本身不算美德。

2. 決定不做決定也算決定。沒能力做決定才是無能。

3. 管理人的存在，有個重要的理由，就是要在政策上做明智的例外。

思想開放的法則：

死也不肯變的人，拒絕不了變壞的誘惑。

Ely 的成功秘訣：

製造需要然後加以滿足。

Bralek 的成功法則：

只信任那些事情出錯還跟著你賠到底的人。

▼THE GOLDEN RULE OF ARTS AND SCIENCES:

Whoever has the gold makes the rules.

▼GUMMIDGE'S LAW:

The amount of expertise varies in inverse proportion to the number of statements understood by the general public.

▼DUNNE'S LAW:

The territory behind rhetoric is too often mined with equivocation.

▼MALEK'S LAW:

Any simple idea will be worded in the most complicated way.

▼ALLISON'S PRECEPT:

The best simple-minded test of expertise in a particular area is the ability to win money in a series of bets on future occurrences in that area.

▼藝文與科學的金科玉律：
　金主講的話就是道理。

▼Gummidge 的定律：
　專業知識的多寡，與大眾聽得懂多少說明成反比。

▼Dunne 的定律：
　巧妙的言詞背後常埋伏著模稜兩可的語法。

▼Malek 的定律：
　最簡單的想法會用最複雜的字眼來說。

▼Allison 的原則：
　要試驗有無真才實學，有個最直率的方法，就
　是以預測這個領域未來會發生什麼事做賭局，
　看能不能贏錢。

POTTER'S LAW:

The amount of flak received on any subject is inversely proportional to the subject's true value.

THE RULE OF THE WAY OUT:

Always leave room to add an explanation if it doesn't work out.

ROSS' LAW:

Never characterize the importance of a statement in advance.

CLARKE'S FIRST LAW:

When a distinguished but elderly scientist states that something is possible, he is almost certainly right. When he states that something is impossible, he is very probably wrong.

CLARKE'S SECOND LAW:

The only way to discover the limits of the possible is to go beyond them into the impossible.

CLARKE'S LAW OF REVOLUTIONARY IDEAS:

Every revolutionary area—in Science, Politics, Art or whatever— evokes three stages of reaction.

They may be summed up by the three phrases:

1. "It is impossible—don't waste my time."

2. "It is possible, but it is not worth doing."

3. "I said it was a good idea all along."

RULE OF THE GREAT:

When somebody you greatly admire and respect appears to be thinking deep thoughts, he or she is probably thinking about lunch.

▼Potter 的定律：
事情所遭受到的反對聲浪，與其真正的價值成反比。

▼解脫法則：
永遠要留有解釋的機會以應付出錯。

▼Ross 的定律：
發表意見以前千萬別說內容有多重要。

▼Clarke 的第一定律：
要是傑出但年事已高的科學家說某事有可能發生，他八成對。要
是他說不可能發生，恐怕就錯了。

▼Clarke 的第二定律：
要知道可行的限度，就走極端做些不可能的事。

▼Clarke 的革命性想法定律：
任何創新的想法——不管在科學、政治、藝術或任何領域——都
有三個反應階段。
這些階段可以總結爲下列三條：
1.「這怎麼可能——別浪費我的時間。」
2.「有可能，不過不值得做。」
3.「我早就說是個好主意嘛。」

▼偉人法則：
你仰慕崇拜的人要是表現出深思的模樣，想的
大概是午餐。

 完全莫非定律

CLARKE'S THIRD LAW:

Any sufficiently advanced technology is indistinguishable from magic.

LAW OF SUPERIORITY:

The first example of superior principle is always inferior to the developed example of inferior principle.

BLAAUW'S LAW:

Established technology tends to persist in spite of new technology.

COHEN'S LAW:

What really matters is the name that you are able to impose upon the facts—not the facts themselves.

FITZ-GIBBON'S LAW:

Creativity varies inversely with the number of cooks involved with the broth.

BARTH'S DISTINCTION:

There are two types of people: those who divide people into two types, and those who don't.

SEGAL'S LAW:

A man with one watch knows what time it is.
A man with two watches is never sure.

MILLER'S LAW:

You can't tell how deep a puddle is until you step in it.

LaCOMBE'S RULE OF PERCENTAGES:

The incidence of anything worthwhile is either 15-25 percent or 80-90 percent.

◥Clarke 的第三定律：

任何高度發展的科技都跟魔術毫無差別。

◥優越定律：

好原則最初的例子，總是比不上壞原則發展完備的範例。

◥Blaauw 的定律：

儘管有新的技術，行之有年的技術依然盛行。

◥Cohen 的定律：

重要的是如何給事情一個指稱的名號——事情本身倒不重要了。

◥Fitz-Gibbon 的定律：

參與的人數與創意成反比。

◥Barth 的分類法：

人有兩種：一種把人分兩種，另一種不這麼分。

◥Segal 的定律：

有一隻錶的人知道現在幾點。

有兩隻錶的人永遠不確定。

◥Miller 的定律：

水窪只有踩進去才知道多深。

◥LaCombe 的百分比法則：

有份量的事情不是在百分之十五到二十五之間，就是在百分之八十到九十之間。

◤Dudenhoefer's Corollary:

An answer of 50 percent will suffice for the 40-60 range.

◤WEILER'S LAW:

Nothing is impossible for the man who doesn't have to do it himself.

◤WEINBERG'S FIRST LAW:

If builders built buildings the way programmers wrote programs, then the first woodpecker that came along would destroy civilization.

◤Weinberg's corollary:

An expert is a person who avoids the small errors while sweeping on to the grand fallacy.

▼Dudenhoefer 以此類推：

答案如果是百分之五十，可適用於四十到六十之間。

▼Weiler 的定律：

不必親自動手的人，總覺得天下無難事。

▼Weinberg 的第一定律：

如果蓋房子的人蓋房子就像做計畫的人做計畫，只要飛來一隻啄木鳥，文明就完蛋了。

▼Weinberg 以此類推：

專家這種人總避開紕漏，直奔大謬。

ADVANCED
EXPERTSMANSHIP

進階專家經

◥MARS' RULE:

An expert is anyone from out of town.

◥WEBER'S DEFINITION:

An expert is one who knows more and more about less and less until they know absolutely everything about nothing.

◥MacDONALD'S LAW:

Consultants are mystical people who ask a company for a number and then give it back to them.

◥WARREN'S RULE:

To spot the expert, pick the one who predicts the job will take the longest and cost the most.

◥WINGER'S RULE:

If it sits on your desk for fifteen minutes, you've just become the expert.

◥SCHROEDER'S LAW:

Indecision is the basis for flexibility.

◥FAGIN'S RULE ON PAST PREDICTION:

Hindsight is an exact science.

◥GREEN'S LAW OF DEBATE:

Anything is possible if you don't know what you're talking about.

◥BURKE'S RULE:

Never create a problem for which you do not have the answer.

◥Corollary:

Create problems for which only you have the answer.

▼Mars 的法則：

遠來的和尚會唸經。

▼Weber 的定律：

專家這種人是對愈來愈少的事，知道得愈來愈多，直到對無關緊要的事無所不知。

▼MacDonald 的定律：

顧問是賣弄玄虛的人，跟企業要個數目，然後再把這個數目提供給企業。

▼Warren 的法則：

要看誰是專家，就看哪個說這工作要耗最多時間、花最多錢。

▼Winger 的法則：

如果一件工作擱在你桌上十五分鐘以上，你也成為專家了。

▼Schroeder 的定律：

猶豫是彈性之母。

▼Fagin 後知後覺法則：

放馬後砲是門一絲不苟的學問。

▼Green 的爭論定律：

只要不知所云，怎麼說都言之成理。

▼Burke 的法則：

沒有答案就別製造問題。

▼以此類推：

不妨製造唯獨你有解答的問題。

◥MATZ'S MAXIM:

A conclusion is the place where you got tired of thinking.

◥LEVY'S FIRST LAW:

No amount of genius can overcome a preoccupation with detail.

◥LEVY'S SECOND LAW:

Only God can make a random selection.

◥BUCY'S LAW:

Nothing is ever accomplished by a reasonable man.

◥DUNLAP'S LAWS OF PHYSICS:

1. Fact is solidified opinion.
2. Facts may weaken under extreme heat and pressure.
3. Truth is elastic.

◥MERKIN'S MAXIM:

When in doubt, predict that the trend will continue.

◥HALGREN'S SOLUTION:

When in trouble, obfuscate.

◥HAWKINS' THEORY OF PROGRESS:

Progress does not consist in replacing a theory that is wrong with one that is right. It consists in replacing a theory that is wrong with one that is more subtly wrong.

◥MEYER'S LAW:

It is a simple task to make things complex, but a complex task to make them simple.

◥HLADE'S LAW:

If you have a difficult task, give it to a lazy man—he will find an easier way to do it.

▼Matz 的格言：

　想到懶得再想，就是結論所在。

▼Levy 的第一定律：

　再高的天份也無法戰勝吹毛求疵。

▼Levy 的第二定律：

　只有上帝才能隨機取樣。

▼Bucy 的定律：

　有史以來理智的人就不曾有過半點成就。

▼Dunlap 的物理定律：

　1.事實是凝固的意見。

　2.在極端的溫度與壓力下，事實也會軟化。

　3.真理有彈性。

▼Merkin 的格言：

　只要不確定，就預言趨勢會持續。

▼Halgren 的解決之道：

　遇到困難就含混其詞。

▼Hawkins 的解決之道：

　所謂進步，不是錯誤的理論給正確的理論取代了。而是錯誤的理
　論給錯得不那麼明顯的理論取代。

▼Meyer 的定律：

　把事情變複雜很簡單，把事情簡化卻很複雜。

▼Hlade 的定律：

　如果手上有件棘手差事，交給懶人就行了——
　懶人一定想得出容易的做法。

ACCOUNTSMANSHIP
精打細算篇

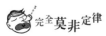
◥ FROTHINGHAM'S FALLACY:

Time is money.

◥ CRANE'S LAW:

There ain't no such thing as a free lunch.

◥ TUCCILLE'S LAW OF REALITY:

Industry always moves in to fill an economic vacuum.

◥ WESTHEIMER'S RULE:

To estimate the time it takes to do a task: estimate the time you think it should take, multiply by two and change the unit of measure to the next highest unit. Thus we allocate two days for a one-hour task.

◥ EDWARDS' TIME/EFFORT LAW:

Effort $\times$ Time = Constant

1. Given a large initial time to do something, the initial effort will be small.
2. As time goes to zero, effort goes to infinity.

Corollary: If it weren't for the last minute, nothing would get done.

◥ GRESHAM'S LAW:

Trivial matters are handled promptly; important matters are never solved.

◥ GRAY'S LAW OF PROGRAMMING:

"N+1" trivial tasks are expected to be accomplished in the same time as "n" tasks.

◥ LOGG'S REBUTTAL TO GRAY'S LAW:

"N+1" trivial tasks take twice as long as "n" trivial tasks.

▼Frothingham 的謬誤：
　時間就是金錢。

▼Crane 的定律：
　天下沒有白吃的午餐。

▼Tuccille 的現實定律：
　經濟一出現眞空狀態，產業總會加以塡補。

▼Westheimer 的法則：
　如何估計工作所需時間：先估計事情該花的時間，乘以二，再把
　計算單位換成次大的單位。於是一個小時的事，我們安排兩天來
　做。

▼Edwards 的時間／工夫定律：
　所花工夫乘以時間等於常數。
　1.任何事情配給大量的時間起步，起步的工夫就花得不多。
　2.時間愈耗愈少，要花的工夫便無限膨脹。
　同理可證：要不是到了最後關頭，什麼事情也不會做。

▼Gresham 的定律：
　瑣事趕著辦，大事放著爛。

▼Gray 的計畫定律：
　大家期望 n＋1 件瑣事與 n 件瑣事的完成時間一
　樣。

▼Logg 反駁 Gray 定律：
　n＋1 件瑣事所花的時間爲 n 件瑣事的一倍。

 完全莫非定律

THE 90/90 RULE OF PROJECT SCHEDULES:

The first 90 percent of the task taskes 90 percent of the time, and the last 10 percent takes the other 90 percent.

WEINBERG'S LAW:

Progress is made on alternate Fridays.

THE ORDERING PRINCIPLE:

Those supplies necessary for yesterday's experiment must be ordered no later than tomorrow noon.

CHEOPS' LAW:

Nothing ever gets built on schedule or within budget.

EXTENDED EPSTEIN-HEISENBERG PRINCIPLE:

In an R&D orbit, only two of the existing three parameters can be defined simultaneously. The parameters are: task, time, and resources.

1. If one knows what the task is, and there is a time limit allowed for the completion of the task, then one cannot guess how much it will cost.

2. If the time and resources are clearly defined, then it is impossible to know what part of the R&D task will be performed.

3. If you are given a clearly defined R&D goal and a definite amount of money that has been calculated to be necessary for the completion of the task, you cannot predict if and when the goal will be reached.

If one is lucky enough and can accurately define all three parameters, then what one deals with is not in the realm of R&D.

▼90/90 的行事曆訂定法則：

前百分之九十的事花掉百分之九十的時間，剩下的百分之十再花百分之九十的時間。

▼Weinberg 的定律：

每兩個星期五進步一次。

▼訂貨原則：

昨天實驗要用的東西，最晚明天中午前要訂好。

▼Cheops 的定律：

建設不是進度落後就是超出預算。

▼Epstein-Heisenberg 的擴充原則：

在研發部門的世界裡，三個參數只有兩個可以同時確定。這三個參數是任務、時間、資金。

1.要是知道任務是什麼，也有個完成的時限，就是不知道要花多少錢。

2.時間和資金都清楚訂定，就是不知道研發計畫的哪一部分要執行。

3.有了明確的研發目標，完成任務必須花的錢也算得清清楚楚了，這時候卻不知道目標什麼時候達成、有沒有辦法達成。

這三個參數要是有幸能精確訂出，那麼處理的事一定不屬於研發這個領域。

PARETO'S LAW (THE 20/80 LAW):

Twenty percent of the customers account for 80 percent of the turnover.

Twenty percent of the components account for 80 percent of the cost.

O'BRIEN'S PRINCIPLE (THE $357.73 THEORY):

Auditors always reject any expense account with a bottom line divisible by five or ten.

ISSAWI'S OBSERVATION ON THE CONSUMPTION OF PAPER:

Each system has its own way of consuming vast amounts of paper: socialist societies fill out large forms in quadruplicate; capitalist societies put up huge posters and wrap every article in four layers of cardboard.

BROWN'S LAW OF BUSINESS SUCCESS:

Our customer's paperwork is profit. Our own paperwork is loss.

JOHN'S COLLATERAL COROLLARY:

In order to get a loan you must first prove you don't need it.

BRIEN'S LAW:

At some time in the life cycle of virtually every organization, its ability to succeed in spite of itself runs out.

LAW OF INSTITUTIONS:

The opulence of the front-office decor varies inversely with the fundamental solvency of the firm.

▼Pareto 的定律（20/80 定律）：
百分之二十的顧客包辦了百分之八十的營業額。
百分之二十的零件花掉了百分之八十的成本。

▼O'Brien 的原則（$357.73 理論）：
凡是費用底限可以用五或十除盡的，審查員無不退回。

▼Issawi 的紙張消耗理論：
每個體系都有自己大量耗紙的方式：社會主義社會用大表格，一
式四份；資本主義社會張貼大型海報，什麼東西都用四層厚紙板
包裝。

▼Brown 的事業成功定律：
客戶的文書作業是利潤。自己的文書作業是虧損。

▼John 的抵押物推論：
想貸款得先證明你不缺錢。

▼Brien 的定律：
幾乎任何組織到了生命週期裡的某個時候，就會把成功的能力用
光。

▼機構定律：
門面豪華的程度，與基本償債能力成反比。

◥PAULG'S LAW:

In America, it's not how much an item costs, it's how much you save.

◥PERLSWEIG'S FIRST LAW:

People who can least afford to pay rent, pay rent.

People who can most afford to pay rent, build up equity.

◥JUHANI'S LAW:

The compromise will always be more expensive than either of the suggestions it is compromising.

▼Paulg 的定律：
　在美國，花多少成本不重要，能省多少才算數。

▼Perlsweig 的第一定律：
　最付不起房租的人得付房租。
　最付得起房租的人房產日增。

▼Juhani 的定律：
　兩項提案達成妥協後，協議的成本只會比原來的提案更高。

DESIGNSMANSHIP

設計經

POULSEN'S PROPHECY:

If anything is used to its full potential, it will break.

MAYNE'S LAW:

Nobody notices the big errors.

PRINCIPLE OF DESIGN INERTIA:

Any change looks terrible at first.

ENG'S PRINCIPLE:

The easier it is to do, the harder it is to change.

WALLACE WOOD'S RULE OF DRAWING:

1. Never draw what you can copy.

2. Never copy what you can trace.

3. Never trace what you can cut out and paste down.

ROBERTSON'S LAW:

Quality assurance doesn't.

WRIGHT'S LAW OF QUALITY:

Quality is inversely proportional to the time left for completion of the project.

LAW OF CORPORATE PLANNING:

Anything that can be changed will be changed until there is no time left to change anything.

GORE'S LAWS OF DESIGN ENGINEERING:

1. The primary function of the design engineer is to make things difficult for the fabricator and impossible for the serviceman.

2. That component of any circuit which has the shortest service life will be placed in the least accessible location.

▼Poulsen 的預言：
　任何裝置開到最大就會壞掉。

▼Mayne 的定律：
　大毛病誰也不會注意到。

▼設計慣性原則：
　任何改變起先看來都可怕。

▼Eng 的原則：
　越容易做的事愈難改。

▼Wallace Wood 的畫圖法則：
　1. 能抄的就別畫。
　2. 能描的就別抄。
　3. 能剪貼的就別描。

▼Robertson 的定律：
　品質無所謂保證。

▼Wright 的品質定律：
　品質與完成方案能用的時間長短成反比。

▼企業規劃定律：
　能改的都會改，直到沒時間再改為止。

▼Gore 的設計工程定律：
　1. 設計師的第一要務，就是讓生產部門頭痛，
　　讓服務部門沒輒。
　2. 任何電路裡使用壽命最短的零件，會放在最
　　難拿的地方。

3. Any circuit design must contain at least one part that is obsolete, two parts that are unobtainable and three parts that are still under development.

Corollary:

    A. The project engineer will change the design to suit the state of the art.

    B. The changes will not be mentioned in the service manual.

◥THE BASIC LAW OF CONSTRUCTION:

Cut it large and kick it into place.

◥MEISSNER'S LAW:

Any producing entity is the last to use its own product.

◥FIRST LAW FOR FREE-LANCE ARTISTS:

A high-paying rush job comes in only after you have committed to a low-paying rush job.

◥SECOND LAW FOR FREE-LANCE ARTISTS:

All rush jobs are due the same day.

◥THIRD LAW FOR FREE-LANCE ARTISTS:

The rush job you spent all night on won't be needed for at least two days.

◥MacPHERSON'S THEORY OF ENTROPY:

It requires less energy to take an object out of its proper place than to put it back.

◥SCHRANK'S FIRST LAW:

If it doesn't work, expand it.

3. 任何電路設計裡，一定有一個零件是過時的，兩個買不到，三個還在研發當中。

同理可證：

    A. 設計工程師會更動設計以配合最新科技發展。

    B. 這些更動不會在服務手冊裡提到。

▼建設的基本定律：
大手筆發狠去幹就成功。

▼Meissner 的定律：
製造業者總是沒東西用才用自己的產品。

▼自由創作者第一定律：
等你接下低報酬的急件，就會有高報酬的急件出現。

▼自由創作者第二定律：
所有急件都同一天截稿。

▼自由創作者第三定律：
你通宵趕出來的急件，至少兩天內都不會來要。

▼MacPherson 的熵理論：
取東西花的能量少於把東西歸位的能量。

▼Schrank 的第一定律：
行不通就擴充。

▼Corollary:

The greater the magnitude, the less notice will be taken that it does not work.

▼BITTON'S POSTULATE ON STATE-OF-THE-ART ELECTRONICS:

If you understand it, it's obsolete.

▼JOSE'S AXIOM:

Nothing is as temporary as that which is called permanent.

▼Corollary:

Nothing is as permanent as that which is called temporary.

▼OSBORN'S LAW:

Variables won't; constants aren't.

▼KLIPSTEIN'S LAW OF SPECIFICATION:

In specifications, Murphy's Law supersedes Ohm's.

▼以此類推：
　愈龐大就愈不會有人注意到行不通。

▼Bitton 的當代電子學原則：

　能懂的就是過時了。

▼Jose 的格言：
　說是永恆的最是轉眼就變。

▼以此類推：
　說是短暫的最是持久不變。

▼Osborn 的定律：
　該變的不變；不該變的變。

▼Klipstein 的說明書定律：
　在說明書裡，莫非定律已取代歐姆定律。

FIRST LAW OF REVISION:

Information necessitating a change of design will be conveyed to the designer after—and only after—the plans are complete. (Often called the "Now They Tell Us!" Law.)

Corollary:

In simple cases, presenting one obvious right way versus one obvious wrong way, it is often wiser to choose the wrong way, so as to expedite subsequent revision.

SECOND LAW OF REVISION:

The more innocuous the modification appears to be, the further its influence will extend and the more plans will have to be redrawn.

THIRD LAW OF REVISION:

If, when completion of a design is imminent, field dimensions are finally supplied as they actually are—instead of as they were meant to be—it is always simpler to start all over.

Corollary:

It is usually impractical to worry beforehand about interferences—if you have none, someone will make one for you.

LAW OF THE LOST INCH:

In designing any type of construction, no overall dimension can be totalled correctly after 4:40 P.M. on Friday.

Corollaries:

1. Under the same conditions, if any minor dimensions are given to sixteenths of an inch, they cannot be totalled at all.
2. The correct total will become self-evident at 9:01 A.M. on Monday.

修改的第一定律：
計畫完成了──也一定要等計畫完成──才會又來些新資料，讓計畫非改不可。（通常也稱做「到這時候才說」定律。）

以此類推：
案子要是簡單，在對與錯的方法之間，不妨選錯的，這樣就可以提前進入修改的步驟。

修改的第二定律：
修改看來愈是輕微，其影響就愈深遠，就有更多計畫必須重訂。

修改的第三定律：
如果設計即將完成，而試車結果並不如預期，那麼重新開始總是比修改簡單。

以此類推：
事前擔心有人干擾通常不切實際──就算沒有干擾，也會有人幫你製造。

失落的尾數定律：
設計任何工程，所有尺寸的總合總是要到週五的下午四點四十分才會算對。

以此類推：
1. 條件相同，凡是涉及十六分之幾英寸的細部，加總後一定不對。
2. 到了星期一早上午九點一分，正確的總數就一目了然。

LAWS OF APPLIED CONFUSION:

1. The one piece that the plant forgot to ship is the one that supports 75 percent of the balance of the shipment.

Corollary: Not only did the plant forget to ship it, 50 percent of the time they haven't even made it.

2. Truck deliveries that normally take one day will take five when you are waiting for the truck.

3. After adding two weeks to the schedule for unexpected delays, add two more for the unexpected, unexpected delays.

4. In any structure, pick out the one piece that should not be mismarked and expect the plant to cross you up.

Corollaries:

   a. In any group of pieces with the same erection mark on it, one should not have that mark on it.

   b. It will not be discovered until you try to put it where the mark says it's supposed to go.

   c. Never argue with the fabricating plant about an error. The inspection prints are all checked off, even to the holes that aren't there.

WYSZKOWSKI'S THEOREM:

Regardless of the units used by either the supplier or the customer, the manufacturer shall use his or her own arbitrary units convertible to those of either the supplier or the customer only by means of weird and unnatural conversion factors.

THE SNAFU EQUATIONS:

1. Given any problem containing "n" equations, there will always be "n+1" unknowns.

▼應用混亂定律：

1. 工廠忘了裝載的某一件貨，會牽涉到這批貨百分之七十五的帳目結餘。

以此類推：別說是忘了裝載，有百分之五十的機率是連做都沒做。

2. 平時卡車運送如果需要花一天，你等的那輛就要花五天才到。

3. 行事曆上加了兩週的意外延遲後，不妨再加兩週意外的意外延遲。

4. 不管在哪個組織裡，要是有哪件事不能弄錯，工廠就一定給你出錯。

以此類推：

a. 如果某一組東西都有同樣的朝上符號，那個符號根本就不該在那裡。

b. 等你照符號要求放置，你才會發現這點。

c. 千萬別跟工廠理論這個錯誤。品管戳記都核對過了，連不存在的坑洞都查過了。

▼Wyszkowski 的理論：

不管供應商或客戶用什麼單位，製造商會用他們自己任意選的單位，而且要怪異或不自然的單位換算，才能換算成供應商或客戶使用單位。

▼Snafu 對等原理：

1. 有 n 個等式的問題總是有 n＋1 個未知數。

2. An object or bit of information most needed will be the least available.

3. Once you have exhausted all possibilities and fail, there will be one solution, simple and obvious, highly visible to everyone else.

4. Badness comes in waves.

SKINNER'S CONSTANT (FLANNAGAN'S FINAGLING FACTOR):

That quantity which, when multiplied by, divided by, added to, or subtracted from the answer you get, gives you the answer you should have gotten.

SHAW'S PRINCIPLE:

Build a system that even a fool can use, and only a fool will want to use it.

LAST LAW OF PRODUCT DESIGN:

If you can't fix it, feature it.

2. 迫切需要的東西或資料總是最不容易取得。

3. 一旦試過所有可能的情形還試不通，就會有個既簡單又明顯的
   解決辦法，大家一眼就看出來。

4. 禍不單行。

▼Skinner 的常數（Flannagan 的取巧因數）：
用這個常數和你得到的答案或加或減或乘或除，就會得到你早該
得到的答案。

▼Shaw 的原則：
建立連傻子都會用的系統，結果就會只有傻子才想用。

▼產品設計的最後定律：
如果搞不定，就描述它的特色。

MACHINESMANSHIP
機械經

IBM POLLYANNA PRINCIPLE:

Machines should work; people should think.

WASHLESKY'S LAW:

Anything is easier to take apart than to put together.

RUDNICKI'S RULE:

That which cannot be taken apart will fall apart.

RAP'S LAW OF INANIMATE REPRODUCTION:

If you take something apart and put it back together enough times, eventually you will have two of them.

BEACH'S LAW:

No two identical parts are alike.

WILLOUGHBY'S LAW:

When you try to prove to someone that a machine won't work, it will.

ANTHONY'S LAW OF THE WORKSHOP:

Any tool, when dropped, will roll into the least accessible corner of the workshop.

Corollary:

On the way to the corner, any dropped tool will first strike your toes.

THE SPARE PARTS PRINCIPLE:

The accessibility, during recovery of small parts that fall from the workbench, varies directly with the size of the part—and inversely with its importance to the completion of the work underway.

▼IBM 樂觀派原則：
　機械應該會動，人應該會想。

▼Washlesky 的定律：
　拆永遠比裝簡單。

▼Rudnicki 的法則：
　拆不開的就會鬆脫。

▼Rap 的非生物生殖定律：
　一件東西不斷拆開拼回，次數夠多了就會變兩件。

▼Beach 的定律：
　同型同號的零件永遠長得不一樣。

▼Willoughby 的定律：
　某台機器壞了，試給別人看的時候竟然就好了。

▼Anthony 的工廠定律：
　工具掉到地上，會滾到廠房裡最難拿的角落。

▼以此類推：
　走過去拿時，工具掉落會先砸到你的腳趾頭。

▼備用零件原則：
　撿取從桌上掉落的小零件，拾得的方便程度與
　該零件大小成正比，與完工的重要程度成反
　比。

SPECIAL LAW:

The workbench is always untidier than last time.

GENERAL LAW:

The chaos in the universe always increases.

FOUR WORKSHOP PRINCIPLES:

1. The one wrench or drill bit you need will be the one missing from the tool chest.
2. Most projects require three hands.
3. Leftover nuts never match leftover bolts.
4. The more carefully you plan a project, the more confusion there is when something goes wrong.

RAY'S RULE FOR PRECISION:

Measure with a micrometer.

Mark with chalk.

Cut with an axe.

LAW OF REPAIR:

You can't fix it if it ain't broke.

RULE OF INTELLIGENT TINKERING:

Save all the parts.

JOHNSON'S LAW:

When any mechanical contrivance fails, it will do so at the most inconvenient possible time.

LAWS OF ANNOYANCE:

When working on a project, if you put away a tool that you're certain you're finished with, you will need it instantly.

▼特別定律：

　工作枱一定比上回亂。

▼一般定律：

　宇宙裡的混亂只增不減。

▼工廠原則四條：

　1. 你需要的板手或鑽子正是工具櫃裡不見的那些。

　2. 大半的工作要三隻手來做。

　3. 剩的螺帽與剩的螺栓永遠不合。

　4. 方案愈是仔細規劃，一旦出錯，情況就愈亂。

▼Ray 的精確法則：

　用細尺量。

　用粉筆標。

　最後用斧頭切。

▼修理定律：

　沒故障的東西修不好。

▼聰明修補法則：

　有備無患。

▼Johnson 的定律：

　機械不靈光，都挑最不巧的時候。

▼煩人定律：

　工作當中，要是哪件工具你肯定不會再用就收
　起來，一定馬上就會用到。

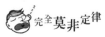

WATSON'S LAW:

The reliability of machinery is inversely proportional to the number and significance of any persons watching it.

WYSZKOWSKI'S LAW:

Anything can be made to work if you fiddle with it long enough.

SATTINGER'S LAW:

It works better if you plug it in.

LOWERY'S LAW:

If it jams—force it. If it breaks, it needed replacing anyway.

THE VCR RULE:

The most expensive special feature on the VCR never gets used.

SCHMIDT'S LAW:

If you mess with a thing long enough, it'll break.

FUDD'S LAW OF OPPOSITION:

Push something hard enough, and it will fall over.

ANTHONY'S LAW OF FORCE:

Don't force it; get a larger hammer.

HORNER'S FIVE-THUMB POSTULATE:

Experience varies directly with equipment ruined.

CAHN'S AXIOM:

When all else fails, read the instructions.

▼Watson 的定律：

　機械的可靠程度，跟旁觀者的數目與重要程度成反比。

▼Wyszkowski 的定律：

　只要花上夠久的時間，什麼東西都弄得好。

▼Sattinger 的定律：

　把插頭插上效果會好些。

▼Lowery 的定律：

　卡住就來硬的。弄壞了換個新的就是。

▼錄影機法則：

　錄影機上最貴的特殊功能向來都用不到。

▼Schmidt 的定律：

　如果你擺弄一個東西夠久，東西就會壞掉。

▼Fudd 的反抗定律：

　催緊了就摧毀了。

▼Anthony 的用力定律：

　別蠻幹，找把大一號的槌子。

▼Horner 的笨拙原則：

　經驗與弄壞的工具成正比。

▼Cahn 的格言：

　什麼辦法都行不通，就看看說明書。

◥THE PRINCIPLE CONCERNING MULTIFUNCTIONAL DEVICES:

The fewer functions any device is required to perform, the more perfectly it can perform those functions.

◥JENKINSON'S LAW:

It won't work.

◥多功能裝置原則：

功能愈少的裝置，運作得愈好。

◥Jenkinson 的定律：

保證沒用。

RESEARCHMANSHIP
研究篇

GORDON'S LAW:

If a research project is not worth doing at all, it is not worth doing well.

MURPHY'S LAW OF RESEARCH:

Enough research will tend to support your theory.

MAIER'S LAW:

If the facts do not conform to the theory, they must be disposed of.

Corollaries:

1. The bigger the theory, the better.
2. The experiment may be considered a success if no more than 50 percent of the observed measurements must be discarded to obtain a correspondence with the theory.

WILLIAMS AND HOLLAND'S LAW:

If enough data are collected, anything may be proven by statistical methods.

EDINGTON'S THEORY:

The number of different hypotheses erected to explain a given biological phenomenon is inversely proportional to the available knowledge.

HARVARD'S LAW:

Under the most rigorously controlled conditions of pressure, temperature, volume, humidity and other variables, the organism will do as it damn well pleases.

▼Gordon 的定律：
　不值得做的研究計畫，就不值得好好做。

▼莫非研究定律：
　實驗做多了理論就成立。

▼Maier 的定律：
　要是結果與理論不合，這樣的結果留不得。

▼以此類推：
　1. 理論愈大愈好。
　2. 如果拋棄不到百分之五十的觀察結果就能使理論成立，那這實
　　　驗就算成功。

▼Williams 和 Holland 的定律：
　資料蒐集夠多了，什麼結果都可以用統計數字證實。

▼Edington 的理論：
　用來解釋某個生物學現象的不同假設的數目，與現有知識的多寡
　成反比。

▼Harvard 的定律：
　在壓力、溫度、數量、溼度等條件及其他變數全都盡全力加以控
　制的情況下，實驗對象愛怎麼反應就怎麼反應。

◣FOURTH LAW OF REVISION:

After painstaking and careful analysis of a sample, you are always told that it is the wrong sample and doesn't apply to the problem.

◣HERSH'S LAW:

Biochemistry expands to fill the space and time available for its completion and publication.

◣FINAGLE'S FIRST LAW:

If an experiment works, something has gone wrong.

◣FINAGLE'S SECOND LAW:

No matter what the anticipated result, there will always be someone eager to (a) misinterpret it, (b) fake it, or (c) believe it happened to their own pet theory.

◣FINAGLE'S THIRD LAW:

In any collection of data, the figure most obviously correct, beyond all need of checking, is the mistake.

▼修正的第四定律：

努力仔細分析了某個樣本，總是會有人跟你說這個樣本不適用於
這個問題。

▼Hersh 的定律：

生物化學會不斷擴充，以填補成書與出版的時間及空間。

▼Finagle 的第一定律：

實驗如果成功，一定是出了什麼錯。

▼Finagle 的第二定律：

不管預期的結果是什麼，總是有人急著：(a)誤解、(b)假造、(c)相
信自己篤信的理論也有同樣的結果。

▼Finagle 的第三定律：

任何蒐集來的資料裡，看起來正確無誤、根本
不需查證的數字，就是錯誤的所在。

Corollaries:

1. No one whom you ask for help will see it.
2. Everyone who stops by with unsought advice will see it immediately.

FINAGLE'S FOURTH LAW:

Once a job is fouled up, anything done to improve it only makes it worse.

FINAGLE'S RULES:

1. To study a subject best, understand it thoroughly before you start.
2. Always keep a record of data—it indicates you're been working.
3. Always draw your curves, then plot your reading.
4. In case of doubt, make it sound convincing.
5. Experiments should be reproducible—they should all fail in the same way.
6. Do not believe in miracles—rely on them.

WINGO'S AXIOM:

All Finagle Laws may be bypassed by learning the simple art of doing without thinking.

RULE OF ACCURACY:

When working toward the solution of a problem, it always helps if you know the answer.

YOUNG'S LAW:

All great discoveries are made by mistake.

Corollary:

The greater the funding, the longer it takes to make the mistake.

▼以此類推：

   1. 你找的救兵都看不出來。

   2. 路過的人不等你問就會挑出來給你看。

▼Finagle 的第四定律：

只要事情搞砸了，什麼補救都只會弄得更糟。

▼Finagle 的法則：

   1. 研究要透澈，著手之前最好完全了解。

   2. 手邊總是要有一份資料記錄──好讓人家覺得你在研究。

   3. 總是先畫曲線再編內容。

   4. 沒把握就要說得跟真的一樣。

   5. 實驗應該可以複製──應該會可以同樣的方式失敗。

   6. 不要相信奇蹟──要依賴。

▼Wingo 的格言：

只要學會光做不想這種簡單的技巧，所有的 Finagle 定律都可以不管。

▼準確法則：

要尋找問題的解決之道，知道答案總是有用。

▼Young 的定律：

所有偉大的發明都是由錯誤造成。

▼以此類推：

籌措愈多資金，就愈久才會犯以上的錯誤。

FETT'S LAW OF THE LAB:

Never replicate a successful experiment.

WYSZOWSKI'S LAW:

No experiment is reproducible.

FUTILITY FACTOR:

No experiment is ever a complete failure—it can always serve as a negative example.

PARKINSON'S LAW OF SCIENTIFIC PROGRESS:

The progress of science varies inversely with the number of journals published.

WHOLE PICTURE PRINCIPLE:

Research scientists are so wrapped up in their own narrow endeavors that they cannot possibly see the whole picture of anything, including their own research.

Corollary:

The Director of Research should know as little as possible about the specific subject of research he or she is administering.

BROOKE'S LAW:

Whenever a system becomes completely defined, some damn fool discovers something that either abolishes the system or expands it beyond recognition.

CAMPBELL'S LAW:

Nature abhors a vacuous experimenter.

FREIVALD'S LAW:

Only a fool can reproduce another fool's work.

▼Fett 的實驗室定律：
千萬別炮製成功的實驗。

▼Wyszowski 的定律：
天下沒有可以複製的實驗。

▼無用因數：
實驗不會一無是處──至少可以當做錯誤的示範。

▼Parkinson 的科學進步定律：
科學進步的速度與論文發表的數量成反比。

▼全貌原則：
從事研究的科學家完全陷在自己的工作裡頭，不可能看清全貌，
包括自己的研究。

▼以此類推：
研發部門主管最好對自己管轄的研究計畫知道的愈少愈好。

▼Brooke 的定律：
每當系統規劃完畢，就會來個該死的傻瓜想出法子，把系統整個
破壞或把系統擴充得面目全非。

▼Campbell 的定律：
大自然最怕沒頭腦的實驗者。

▼Freivald 的定律：
只有傻瓜才有辦法重複傻瓜做的事。

TENENBAUM'S LAW OF REPLICABILITY:

The most interesting results happen only once.

SOUDER'S LAW:

Repetition does not establish validity.

HANGGI'S LAW:

The more trivial your research, the more people will read it and agree.

Corollary:

The more vital your research, the less people will understand it.

HANDY GUIDE TO MODERN SCIENCE:

1. If it's green or it wriggles, it's biology.
2. If it stinks, it's chemistry.
3. If it doesn't work, it'ts physics.

CERF'S EXTENSIONS TO THE HANDY GUIDE TO MODERN SCIENCE:

4. If it's incomprehensible, it's mathematics.
5. If it doesn't make sense, it't either economics or psychology.

YOUNG'S COMMENT ON SCIENTIFIC METHOD:

You can't get here from there.

MACBETH'S COMMENT ON EVOLUTION:

The best theory is not *ipso facto* a good theory.

BARR'S INERTIAL PRINCIPLE:

Asking scientists to revise their theory is like asking cops to revise the law.

▼Tenenbaum 的複製難易定律：
最有意思的結果只出現一次。

▼Souder 的定律：
一再出現不表示成立。

▼Hanggi 的定律：
研究的內容愈是瑣碎，就有愈多人讀了便同意。

▼以此類推：
研究的內容愈是事關重大，懂的人就愈少。

▼現代科學的簡易指南：
1. 綠色或者會扭動的就是生物學。
2. 有臭味就是化學。
3. 行不通的就是物理。

▼Cerf 補充現代科學的簡易指南：
4. 沒人懂的就是數學。
5. 沒道理的不是經濟學就是心理學。

▼Young 評科學方法：
方法由不得你自訂。

▼Macbeth 評演化：
最好的理論，本身實際上不是好理論。

▼Barr 的慣性原則：
要求科學家修正自己的理論，就像要求警察修
正法律。

THE SAGAN FALLACY:

To say a human being being is nothing but molecules is like saying a Shakespearean play is nothing but words.

EINSTEIN'S OBSERVATION:

Inasmuch as the mathematical theorems are related to reality, they are not sure; inasmuch as they are sure, they are not related to reality.

THE RELIABILITY PRINCIPLE:

The difference between the Laws of Nature and Murphy's Law is that with the Laws of Nature you can count on things screwing up the same way every time.

DARWIN'S LAW:

Nature will tell you a direct lie if she can.

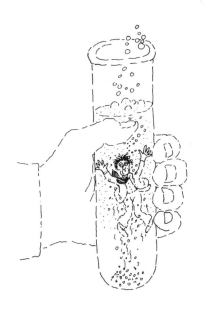

▼沙岡謬論：
把人類視爲一堆分子，就如同說莎士比亞的劇本不過是一堆字。

▼愛因斯坦的心得：
數學定理與現實世界有關連的地方，他們不確定；他們能確定的
部分，肯定與現實世界無關。

▼可靠度原則：
大自然的定律與莫非定律的差別如下：依照大自然的定律，你可
以期待每次事情搞砸的方式都一樣。

▼達爾文定律：
大自然在能說謊處絕不遲疑。

◣BLOCH'S EXTENSION:

So will Darwinists.

◣FIRST LAW OF SCIENTIFIC PROGRESS:

The advance of science can be measured by the rate at which exceptions to previously held laws accumulate.

◣Corollaries:

1. Exceptions always outnumber rules.
2. There are always exceptions to established exceptions.
3. By the time one masters the exceptions, no one recalls the rules to which they apply.

◣FIRST LAW OF PARTICLE PHYSICS:

The shorter the life of the particle, the more it costs to produce.

◣SECOND LAW OF PARTICLE PHYSICS:

The basic building blocks of matter do not occur in nature.

◣FINMAN'S LAW OF MATHEMATICS:

Nobody wants to read anyone else's formulas.

◣GOLOMB'S DON'SS OF MATHEMATICAL MODELING:

1. Don't believe the thirty-third-order consequences of a first-order model.
   CATCH PHRASE: *"Cum grano salis."*
2. Don't extrapolate beyond the region of fit.
   CATCH PHRASE: "Don't go off the deep end."
3. Don't apply any model until you understand the simplifying assumptions on which it is based, and can test their applicability.
   CATCH PHRASE: "Use only as directed."

▼Bloch 的補充：
　達爾文的信徒也一樣。

▼科學進步的第一定律：
　要測量科學進步，端看行之有年的定律累積了多少例外。

▼以此類推：
　1. 例外永遠多於法則。
　2. 視為當然的例外總是會出現例外。
　3. 等大家都精通這些例外，無人會再想起當初這例外所屬的法
　　　則。

▼分子物理第一定律：
　分子的壽命愈短，製造的成本愈高。

▼分子物理第二定律：
　這些造物的基本建材在自然界裡找不到。

▼Finman 的數學定律：
　誰也不想看別人的公式。

▼Golomb 的數學模型戒律：
　1. 別相信用一階模型求出的三十三階的結果。
　　　口訣：別太管字面意義。
　2. 推測要在適度的範圍之內。
　　　口訣：別魯莽行事。
　3. 任何模型必須先了解模型是建立在怎樣的簡
　　　化基礎上，而且測試其可用程度，這些做完
　　　才可以採用。
　　　口訣：一切依指示行事。

4. Don't believe that the model is the reality.

   CATCH PHRASE: "Don't eat the menu."

5. Don't distort reality to fit the model.

   CATCH PHRASE: "The 'Procrustes Method.' "

6. Don't limit yourself to a single model: more than one may be useful for understanding different aspects of the same phenomenon.

   CATCH PHRASE: "Legalize polygamy."

7. Don't retain a discredited model.

   CATCH PHRASE: "Don't beat a dead horse."

8. Don't fall in love with your model.

   CATCH PHRASE: "Pygmalion."

9. Don't apply the terminology of Subject A to the problems of Subject B if it is to the enrichment of neither.

   CATCH PHRASE: "New names for old."

10. Don't expect that by having named a demon you have destroyed him.

    CATCH PHRASE: "Rumpelstiltskin."

◥LAW OF LABORATORY WORK:

Hot glass looks exactly the same as cold glass.

◥FELSON'S LAW:

To steal ideas from one person is plagiarism; to steal from many is research.

◥VALERY'S LAW:

History is the science of what never happens twice.

◥DARROW'S COMMENT ON HISTORY:

History repeats itself. That's one of the things wrong with history.

4. 別以爲模型就是眞實狀況。

　　□訣：別吃菜單。

5. 別扭曲事實以牽就模型。

　　□訣：削足適履。

6. 別把自己局限在一個模型裡：許多模型都有助於了解一個現象的不同層面。

　　□訣：一夫多妻該合法化。

7. 別保留有瑕疵的模型。

　　□訣：別醫死馬。

8. 別愛上自己的模型。

　　□訣：自戀狂。

9. 要是把 A 主題的術語應用到 B 主題，尙無法使雙方更爲豐富，就別這麼做。

　　□訣：舊酒裝新瓶。

10. 別夢想將禍害命名就等於將其消滅。

　　□訣：Rumpelstilstskin（德國的民間傳說人物，因名字被猜中而自殺）。

▼**實驗室工作定律：**

玻璃杯不管冷熱看起來都一個樣。

▼**Felson 的定律：**

偷一個人的想法叫做剽竊，偷許多人的想法叫研究。

▼**Valery 的定律：**

歷史是絕不重演的科學。

▼**Darrow 評歷史：**

歷史一再重演。這是歷史的壞處之一。

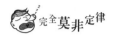

◥PRIMARY RULE OF HISTORY:

History doesn't repeat itself—historians merely repeat each other.

◥PAVLU'S RULES FOR ECONOMY IN RESEARCH:

1. Deny the last established truth on the list.
2. Add yours.
3. Pass the list.

◥MR. COOPER'S LAW:

If you do not understand a particular word in a piece of technical writing, ignore it. The piece will make perfect sense without it.

◥BOGOVICH'S COROLLARY TO MR. COOPER'S LAW:

If the piece makes no sense without the word, it will make no sense with the word.

◥GROUND RULE FOR LABORATORY WORKERS:

When you do not know what you are doing, do it neatly.

◥FINAGLE'S RULE:

Teamwork is essential. It allows you to blame someone else.

◥FINAGLE'S CREED:

Science is true. Don't be misled by facts.

◥MUENCH'S LAW:

Nothing improves an innovation like lack of controls.

◥MAY'S LAW OF STRATIGRAPHY:

The quality of correlation is inversely proportional to the density of control.

▼歷史首要法則：

歷史不會重演——只是史學家相互抄襲。

▼Pavlu 的研究經濟法則：

1. 否定清單上最近才建立的原理。

2. 加上自己的創見。

3. 把清單傳下去。

▼Cooper 先生的定律：

如果科技文章上有哪個特殊名詞不懂，別理它。沒它一樣說得通。

▼Bogovich 類推 Cooper 先生定律：

如果該篇去掉某個名詞就沒意義，那麼有那個名詞一樣沒意義。

▼實驗室工作人員的基本法則：

如果不知道自己在做什麼，就做得乾淨俐落些。

▼Finagle 的法則：

團隊合作十分重要。這樣才可以怪別人。

▼Finagle 的信條：

科學是真理。別讓事實誤導了。

▼Muench 的定律：

缺乏管制最能讓改革更上層樓。

▼May 的地層學定律：

默契與管制的密度成反比。

完全莫非定律

VESILIND'S LAW OF EXPERIMENTATION:

1. If reproducibility may be a problem, conduct the test only once.

2. If a straight line fit is required, obtain only two data points.

LERMAN'S LAW OF TECHNOLOGY:

Any technical problem can be overcome given enough time and money.

Lerman's Corollary:

You are never given enough time or money.

ROCKY'S LEMMA OF INNOVATION PREVENTION:

Unless the results are known in advance, funding agencies will reject the proposal.

THUMB'S FIRST POSTULATE:

It is better to solve a problem with a crude approximation and know the truth, plus or minus 10 percent, than to demand an exact solution and not know the truth at all.

THUMB'S SECOND POSTULATE:

An easily understood, workable falsehood is more useful than a complex, incomprehensible truth.

JONES' LAW:

Anyone who makes a significant contribution to any field of endeavor, and stays in that field long enough, becomes an obstruction to its progress—in direct proportion to the importance of the original contribution.

▼Vesilind 的實驗定律：

　1. 測試如果難以重複，就只做一次。

　2. 如果只要求合於直線，那麼就只求出兩個資料點。

▼Lerman 的技術定律：

　一切技術問題只要花夠多的時間與金錢都能解決。

▼Lerman 加以類推：

　時間與金錢向來不夠。

▼Rocky 預防改革的補助定理：

　除非事先能知道結果，否則出錢的單位會把提案退回。

▼Thumb 的第一教訓：

　解決問題最好是用個概略的方法求出解答，再加減個百分之十，
　不要只求精確的解決方法，而根本求不出解答。

▼Thumb 的第二教訓：

　易懂可用的假象勝過複雜難懂的真象。

▼Jones 的定律：

　誰要是在哪個領域裡有重大貢獻又待得夠久，就會成為進步的障
　礙──跟當初貢獻的重要性成正比。

MANN'S LAW (generalized):

If a scientist uncovers a publishable fact, it will become central to his theory.

Corollary:

His theory, in turn, will become central to all scientific thought.

THE RULER RULE:

There is no such thing as a straight line.

GRELB'S LAW OF ERRORING:

In any series of calculations, errors tend to occur at the opposite end from which you begin checking.

ROBERT'S AXIOM:

Only errors exist.

Berman's Corollary to Robert's Axiom:

One man's error is another man's data.

◥Mann的定律（普及版）：

科學家要是發現了可供出版的事實，就成爲其理論的中心。

◥以此類推：

他的理論到時候又成爲所有科學思想的中心。

◥尺的法則：

天底下沒有直線這東西。

◥Grelb的犯錯定律：

檢查任何一連串計算過程，不管你從哪端開始檢查，錯誤大半在另一端。

◥Robert的格言：

錯誤常存。

◥Berman類推Robert的格言：

某甲的錯誤是某乙的資料。

COMPUTER MURPHOLOGY
電腦莫非學篇

LAW OF UNRELIABILITY:

To err is human, but to really foul things up requires a computer.

GREER'S LAW:

A computer program does what you tell it to do, not what you want it to do.

SUTIN'S LAW:

The most useless computer tasks are the most fun to do.

McCRISTY'S COMPUTER AXIOMS:

1. Back-up files are never complete.
2. Software bugs are correctable only after the software is judged obsolete by the industry.

LEO BEISER'S COMPUTER AXIOM:

When putting it into memory, remember where you put it.

STEINBACH'S GUIDELINE FOR SYSTEMS PROGRAMMING:

Never test for an error condition you don't know how to handle.

MANUBAY'S LAWS FOR PROGRAMMERS:

1. If a programmer's modification of an existing program works, it's probably not what the users want.
2. Users don't know what they really want, but they know for certain what they don't want.

LAWS OF COMPUTER PROGRAMMING:

1. Any given program, when running, is obsolete.
2. Any given program costs more and takes longer.
3. If a program is useful, it will have to be changed.
4. If a program is useless, it will have to be documented.

▼不可靠定律：
　人沒有不犯錯的，不過要把事情搞砸就需要電腦。

▼Greer 的定律：
　電腦只做你叫它做的，而不是你想要它做的。

▼Sutin 的定律：
　最沒用處的電腦任務最有趣。

▼McCristy 的電腦格言：
　1.備份總是不全。
　2.軟體的病毒要等到這個軟體公認過時了才治得好。

▼Leo Beiser 的電腦格言：
　儲存時要記得存在哪兒。

▼Steinbach 的系統設計指南：
　不知道如何處理的誤差狀態，就千萬別加以測試。

▼Manubay 的程式設計師定律：
　1. 如果程式設計師對現有程式的修正行得通，那大半不符使用者
　　需求。
　2. 使用者不知道自己要什麼，不過他們很清楚不要什麼。

▼電腦程式設計定律：
　1. 凡是程式，能跑的都是過時的。
　2. 凡是程式都得花更多錢、更多時間。
　3. 有用的程式就一定需要修改。
　4. 沒用的程式就必須列入文件檔案。

5. Any given program will expand to fill all available memory.

6. The value of a program is proportional to the weight of its output.

7. Program complexity grows until it exceeds the capability of the programmer who must maintain it.

TROUTMAN'S PROGRAMMING POSTULATES:

1. If a test installation functions perfectly, all subsequent systems will malfunction.

2. Not until a program has been in production for at least six months will the most harmful error be discovered.

3. Job control cards that positively cannot be arranged in improper order will be.

4. Interchangeable tapes won't.

5. If the input editor has been designed to reject all bad input, an ingenious idiot will discover a method to get bad data past him or her.

6. Profanity is the one language all programmers know best.

GILB'S LAWS OF UNRELIABILITY:

1. Computers are unreliable, but humans are even more unreliable.

2. Any system that depends on human reliability is unreliable.

3. Undetectable errors are infinite in variety, in contrast to detectable errors, which by definition are limited.

4. Investment in reliability will increase until it exceeds the probable cost of errors, or until someone insists on getting some useful work done.

BROOK'S LAW:

Adding manpower to a late software project makes it later.

5. 只要是程式都會把記憶體填滿。

6. 程式的價值與其輸出的重量成正比。

7. 程式會愈來愈複雜,直到讓負責的維修人員也束手無策爲止。

▼Troutman 的程式設計原則:

1. 如果起動測試進行順利,隨後的所有系統都會出錯。

2. 程式一定要等生產六個月以後,殺傷力最強的錯誤才會出現。

3. 應該條理分明的作業控制卡,偏偏排亂了。

4. 可以替換的帶子偏不能替換。

5. 輸入系統介面若有過濾不良輸入的職責,就會有個聰明的白癡
   想出偷渡壞資訊的方法。

6. 髒話是所有程式設計者都精通的語言。

▼Gilb 的不可靠定律:

1. 電腦不可靠,人類更加不可靠。

2. 系統若得依賴人類的可靠度,就不可靠。

3. 可偵測的錯誤本來就很有限,相形之下不可偵測的錯誤就變化
   萬千。

4. 改善系統穩定性的投資會一再追加,直到比預估失誤的花費更
   高,或是有人堅持改做點有效益的事。

▼Brook 的定律:

軟體計畫進度落後的話,再增加人力只會更
慢。

完全莫非定律

◥LAWS OF COMPUTERDOM ACCORDING TO GOLUB:

1. Fuzzy project objectives are used to avoid the embarrassment of estimating the corresponding costs.
2. A carelessly planned project takes three times longer to complete than expected; a carefully planned project takes only twice as long.
3. The effort required to correct course increases geometrically with time.
4. Project teams detest weekly progress reporting because it so vividly displays their lack of progress.

◥SMITH'S LAW OF COMPUTER REPAIR:

Access holes will be half an inch too small.

◥Corollary:

Holes that are the right size will be in the wrong place.

◥JARUK'S LAW:

If it would be cheaper to buy a new unit, the company will insist upon repairing the old one.

◥Corollary:

If it would be cheaper to repair the old one, the company will insist on the latest model.

◥WEINBERG'S FIRST LAW:

If builders built buildings the way programmers wrote programs, then the first woodpecker that came along would destroy civilization.

◥LUBARSKY'S LAW OF CYBERNETIC ENTOMOLOGY:

There's always one more bug.

▼Golub 所提之電腦國度定律：

1. 模稜二可的計畫目標，常用來避免計算成本時得面對的尷尬。
2. 計畫欠周詳的方案要花三倍預期的時間來完成，計畫周詳的只需兩倍。
3. 改變程序所需的工夫，隨時間成幾何級數增加。
4. 計畫小組討厭每週的進度報告，因為報告清楚顯露了他們的不長進。

▼Smith 的電腦維修定律：

輸入孔會小半吋。

▼以此類推：

大小適當的孔會安錯地方。

▼Jaruk 的定律：

如果買新的比較划算，公司就會堅持修理舊的。

▼以此類推：

如果修理舊的比較划算，公司就會堅持買新機型。

▼Weinberg 的第一定律：

如果人類蓋房子像程式設計師寫程式那樣，那麼第一隻啄木鳥出現時，文明早就毀了。

▼Lubarsky 的人工電腦學昆蟲定律：

總是漏掉一隻病毒。

ACADEMIOLOGY
學院篇

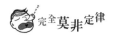 完全莫非定律

H.L. MENCKEN'S LAW:

Those who can, do.

Those who cannot, teach.

Martin's Extension:

Those who cannot teach, administrate.

ELLARD'S LAW:

Those who want to learn will learn.

Those who do not want to learn will lead enterprises.

Those incapable of either learning or leading will regulate scholarship and enterprise to death.

MEREDITH'S LAW FOR GRAD SCHOOL SURVIVAL:

Never let your major professor know that you exist.

VILE'S LAW FOR EDUCATORS:

No one is listening until you make a mistake.

VILE'S LAW OF GRADING PAPERS:

All papers after the top are upside down or backwards, until you right the pile. Then the process repeats.

WEINER'S LAW OF LIBRARIES:

There are no answers, only cross-references.

LAWS OF CLASS SCHEDULING:

1. If the course you wanted most has room for "n" students, you will be the "n+1" o apply.
2. Class schedules are designed so that every student will waste maximum time between classes.

H.L. Mencken 的定律：

行的人做。

不行的人教。

Martin 的引申：

不會教的人管。

Ellard 的定律：

想學的就會學。

不想學的就去領導企業。

那些既學不動又沒有能力領導企業的，就把學術與校務管得死死的。

Meredith 的研究所求生定律：

別讓指導教授知道有你這個人。

Vile 的教書定律：

上課沒人聽，一教錯就有人聽。

Vile 的報告評分定律：

最上面那份報告底下的所有報告，不是上下顛倒就是背面朝上，你得把整堆弄好。接著舊戲又重演。

Weiner 的圖書館定律：

永遠找不到答案，只找得到另一本參考書目。

選課定律：

1. 如果你最想修的課收 n 位學生，你會是第 n+1 個選課的人。

2. 課表的安排總讓學生在兩門課中間浪費最多
   時間。

Corollary: When you are occasionally able to schedule two classes in a row, they will be held inclassrooms at opposite ends of the campus.

3. A prerequisite for a desired course will be offered only during the semester following the desired course.

LAWS OF APPLIED TERROR:

1. When reviewing your notes before an exam, the most important ones will be illegible.

2. The more studying you did for the exam, the less sure you are as to which answer they want.

3. Eighty percent of the final exam will be based on the one lecture you missed about the one book you didn't read.

4. The night before the English history midterm, your Biology instructor will assign two hundred pages on planaria.

Corollary: Every instructor assumes that you have nothing else to do except study for that instructor's course.

5. If you are given an open-book exam, you will forget your book.

Corollary: If you are given a take-home exam, you will forget where you live.

以此類推：如果偶爾走運能把兩門課接連排下來，那麼教室一定
　　　　　分別在校園兩個離得最遠的角落。

3. 修某門課之前必須先修的課，一定只排在那門課之後的那個學
　期。

▼實用恐怖定律：

1. 考試前看筆記，最重要的部分一定字跡潦草。

2. 讀得愈多，愈拿不定標準答案是哪個。

3. 期末考百分之八十的考題都出自你翹掉的那一堂課，上的是你
　沒讀的那一本書。

4. 歷史期中考前一天晚上，生物學老師就會出兩百頁的渦蟲學作
　業。

以此類推：每個老師都以為學生除了自己這門課，沒別的事好
　　　　　做。

5. 如果考試可以翻書，書就忘了帶。

同理可證：如果老師要你們把考卷帶回家寫，
　　　　　你會忘了住在哪兒。

6. At the end of the semester you will recall having enrolled in a course at the beginning of the semester—and never attending.

FIRST LAW OF FINAL EXAMS:

Pocket calculator batteries that have lasted all semester will fail during the math final.

Corollary: If you bring extra batteries, they will be defective.

SECOND LAW OF FINAL EXAMS:

In your toughest final, the most distractingly attractive student in class will sit next to you for the first time.

SEEGER'S LAW:

Anything in parentheses can be ignored.

NATALIE'S LAW OF ALGEBRA:

You never catch on until after the test.

SEIT'S LAW OF HIGHER EDUCATION:

The one course you must take to graduate will not be offered during your last semester.

MURPHY'S RULE OF THE TERM PAPER:

The book or periodical most vital to the completion of your term paper will be missing from the library.

Corollary: If it is available, the most important page will be torn out.

DUGGAN'S LAW OF SCHOLARY RESEARCH:

The most valuable quotation will be the one for which you cannot determine the source.

Corollary: The source for an unattributed quotation will appear in the most hostile review of your work.

6. 學期末你才會想起學期初選了某門課——而且從來沒去上。

期末考第一定律：

口袋型計算機的電池一整學期都沒問題，期末考時卻沒電。

以此類推：如果你帶了備用電池，一定也失效。

期末考第二定律：

考期末考裡最難的一科時，班上那位萬人迷竟首次坐在你身邊。

Seeger 的定律：

括號裡的東西都可以不管。

Natalie 的代數定律：

考完才趕得上進度。

Seit 的高等教育定律：

修過才能畢業的課，一定得等到最後一學期才開。

學期報告的莫非法則：

寫報告最重要的那本書或者期刊，在圖書館裡就是找不到。

以此類推：就算找到了，最重要的一頁已被撕走。

Duggan 的學術研究定律：

最有用的引證就是不確定出處的那條。

以此類推：沒列出處的引證，一定會出現在把
你罵得最慘的那份書評裡。

ROMINGER'S RULES FOR STUDENTS:

1. The more general the title of a course, the less you will learn from it.
2. The more specific a title is, the less you will be able to apply it later.

HANSEN'S LIBRARY AXIOM:

The closest library doesn't have the material you need.

LONDON'S LAW OF LIBRARIES:

No matter which book you need, it's on the bottom shelf.

ATWOOD'S COROLLARY:

No books are lost by lending except those you particularly want to keep.

JOHNSON'S LAW:

If you miss one issue of any magazine, it will be the issue that contained the article, story or installment you were most anxious to read.

Corollary: All of your friends either missed it, lost it or threw it out.

WHITTINGTON'S LAW OF COMMUNICATION:

When a writer prepares a manuscript on a subject he or she does not understand, the work will be understood only by readers who know more about that subject than the writer does.

Corollary: Writings prepared without understanding must fail in the first objective of communication—informing the uninformed.

▼Rominger 的學生法則：
1. 課程名稱愈籠統，學到的東西愈少。
2. 課程名稱愈明確，以後就愈難應用。

▼Hansen 的圖書館通則：
離家最近的圖書館沒有你要的資料。

▼London 的圖書館定律：
你要的書都放在架子底層。

▼Atwood 的類推：
書借人一般不會丟，你特別喜歡的才會丟。

▼Johnson 的定律：
如果哪期雜誌丟了，那期就有你最急著讀的文章、故事、連載小說。

以此類推：你所有朋友訂的那期也都沒來、不見了或丟棄了。

▼Whittington 的溝通定律：
每當有人撰寫自己不懂的主題，這篇文章只有懂得比作者多的人看得懂。

以此類推：自己不懂就寫的文章，一定無法達成溝通的首要目的，就是讓不知道的人知道。

◥KERR-MARTIN LAW:

1. In dealing with their own problems, faculty members are the most extreme conservatives.

2. In dealing with other people's problems, they are the most extreme's iberals.

◥ROMINGER'S RULES FOR TEACHERS:

1. When a student asks for a second time if you have read his book report, he did not read the book.

2. If attendance is mandatory, a scheduled exam will produce increased absenteeism. If attendance is optional, an exam will produce persons you have never seen before.

Kerr-Martin 定律：

1. 校方處理自己的問題極端保守。
2. 校方處理別人的問題極端自由。

Rominger 的教師法則：

1. 如果學生再次問你到底有沒有看他的讀書報告，他一定沒看書。
2. 如果上課必點名，定期小考就會少來一些人。如果上課不點，考試的時候就會出現你從來沒見過的人。

WORK AND OFFICE MURPHOLOGY

工作與辦公室篇

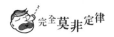

◥ HARDIN'S LAW:

You can never do just one thing.

◥ HECHT'S LAW:

There no time like the present for postponing what you don't ant to do.

◥ GROSSMAN'S LEMMA:

Any task worth doing was worth doing yesterday.

◥ KNAGG'S DERIVATIVE OF MURPHY'S LAW:

The more complicated and grandiose the plan, the greater the chance of failure.

◥ DEHAY'S AXIOM:

Simple jobs always get put off because there will be time to do them later.

◥ WETHERN'S LAW OF SUSPENDED JUDGMENT:

Assumption is the mother of all screw-ups.

◥ KRANSKE'S LAW:

Beware of a day in which you don't have something to bitch about.

◥ PARKINSON'S FIRST LAW:

Work expands to fill the time available for its completion; the thing to be done swells in perceived importance and complexity in a direct ratio with the time to be spent in its completion.

◥ PARKINSON'S SECOND LAW:

Expenditures rise to meet income.

◥ PARKINSON'S THIRD LAW:

Expansion means complexity and complexity decays.

▼Hardin 的定律：
你永遠不可能只做一件事。

▼Hecht 的定律：
不想做的事，現在不停還等什麼時候？

▼Grossman 的難題：
值得做的事都值得昨天做。

▼Knagg 引申莫非定律：
計畫愈複雜、愈冠冕堂皇，失敗的機會愈大。

▼Dehay 的格言：
簡單的事情總是給擱著，反正以後會有時間做。

▼Wethern 的判而不斷力定律：
假設為烏龍之母。

▼Kranske 的定律：
哪天要是沒什麼東西好抱怨，千萬要當心。

▼Parkinson 的第一定律：
工作自然而然佔去所有可用的時間；該做的事，其完成時間愈長，表現出來的重要性與複雜程度也跟著膨脹。

▼Parkinson 的第二定律：
支出會趕上收入。

▼Parkinson 的第三定律：
擴張增加複雜，而複雜造成腐敗。

完全莫非定律

▼PARKINSON'S FOURTH LAW:

The number of people in any working group tends to increase regardless of the amount of work to be done.

▼THE EINSTEIN EXTENSION OF PARKINSON'S LAW:

A work project expands to fill the space available.

Corollary: No matter how large the work space, if two projects must be done at the same time they will require the use of the same part of the work space.

▼SIX LAWS OF OFFICE MURPHOLOGY:

1. Important letters that contain no errors will develop errors in the mail.

Corollary: Corresponding errors will show up in duplicate while the boss is reading it.

2. Office machines that function perfectly during normal business hours will break down when you return to the office at night to use them for personal business.

3. Machines that have broken down will work perfectly when the person who repairs them arrives.

4. Envelopes and stamps that don't stick when you lick them will stick to other things when you don't want them to.

5. Vital papers will demonstrate their vitality by moving from where you left them to where you can't find them.

6. The last person who quit or was fired will be held responsible for everything that goes wrong—until the next person quits or is fired.

▼BOGOVICH'S LAW:

He who hesitates is probably right.

▼Parkinson 的第四定律：
　任何工作團體，不管工作量如何，人數都會增加。

▼愛因斯坦引申 Parkinson 的定律：
　工作計畫會把可用空間塞滿。
　以此類推：不管工作空間有多大，如果有兩件計畫必須同時進
　　　　　　　行，兩者正好需要使用同一個角落。

▼辦公室莫非定律六則：
　1.沒有錯誤的重要信函，在郵寄時會自動生出錯誤。
　以此類推：老闆看副本時，同樣的錯誤也會跑出來。
　2.辦公室的設備在正常工作時間運作順暢，晚上你回辦公室做點私
　　人的事時就會故障。
　3.故障的機器等維修人員一來又恢復正常。
　4.信封和郵票要貼時黏不住，不要它們黏時卻會和其他東西黏在一
　　起。
　5.重要文件為了向你展示其重要，會從你存放文件的地方跑到你找
　　不到的地方。
　6.一切過錯都會歸給上一個辭職或者遭到開除的人──直到又有人
　　辭職或遭到開除。

▼Bogovich 的定律：
　猶豫的人恐怕才對。

◣DEVRIES' DILEMMA:

If you hit two keys on the typewriter, the one you don't want hits the paper.

◣THEORY OF SELECTIVE SUPERVISION:

The one time in the day that you lean back and relax is the one time the boss walks through the office.

◣LAUNEGAYER'S OBSERVATION:

Asking dumb questions is easier than correcting dumb mistakes.

◣STRANO'S LAW:

When all else fails, try the boss't suggestion.

◣BRINTNALL'S LAW:

If you are given two contradictory orders, obey them both.

◣SHAPIRO'S LAW OF REWARD:

The one who does the least work will get the most credit.

◣LAWS OF PROCRASTINATION:

1. shortens the job and places the responsibility for its termination on someone else (the authority who imposed the deadline).
2. It reduces anxiety by reducing the expected quality of the project from the best of all possible efforts to the best that can be expected given the limited time.
3. Status is gained in the eyes of others, and in one's own eyes, because it is assumed that the importance of the work justifies the stress.
4. Avoidance of interruptions, including the assignment of other duties, can usually be achieved, so that the obviously stressed worker can concentrate on the single effort.

◥Devries 的難題：

如果打字同時按了兩個鍵，不要的會打到紙上。

◥選擇性監督原則：

難得靠在椅背上鬆口氣，老闆就來辦公室巡視。

◥Launegayer 的觀察：

問笨問題比糾正笨錯誤簡單。

◥Strano 的定律：

什麼法子都行不通，不妨試試老闆的。

◥Brintnall 的定律：

如果收到兩個相互衝突的指示，兩個都照辦。

◥Shapiro 的報酬定律：

事情做最少的人功勞最大。

◥拖延定律：

1. 拖延能縮減工作量，把完工的責任推給別人（訂出期限的那個主管）。

2. 拖延把計畫所預定的品質，從盡全力所能做到的，降到有限時間內所能做到的，也就是壓力減輕了。

3. 身份地位可以從別人的看法中獲得，不過也可以由自己的看法裡獲得，因為工作若是重要，有壓力也是應該的。

4. 干擾通常可以避免，包括不再接其他任務，所以壓力大的員工就可以只做一件事。

5. Procrastination avoids boredom; one never has the feeling that there is nothing important to do.

6. It may eliminate the job if the need to procrastinate passes before the job can be done.

◥QUILE'S CONSULTATION LAW:

The job that pays the most will be offered when there is no time to deliver the services.

◥DOANE'S LAWS OF PROCRASTINATION:

1. The more proficient one is at procrastination, the less proficient one need be at all else.

2. The slower one works, the fewer mistakes one makes.

◥DREW'S LAW OF PROFESSIONAL PRACTICE:

The client who pays the least complains the most.

◥JOHNSON'S LAW:

The number of minor illnesses among the employees is inversely proportional to the health of the organization.

5. 拖延可以避免無聊；誰也不會覺得沒有要事要辦。

6. 如果工作還沒做完之前就失去拖延的必要，那這件事也就不用
   做了。

▼Quile 的諮詢定律：

錢最多的案子會在沒時間應付時進來。

▼Doane 的拖延定律：

1. 愈會拖的人，愈不需要會做別的事。

2. 做得愈慢錯得愈少。

▼Drew 的專業操作定律：

錢給最少的客戶抱怨最多。

▼Johnson 的定律：

員工微恙的數目與組織的健康成反比。

完全莫非定律

TILLIS' ORGANIZATIONAL PRINCIPLE:

If you file it, you'll know where it is but never need it.

If you don't file it, you'll need it but never know where it is.

OWEN'S LAW FOR SECRETARIES:

As soon as you sit down to a cup of hot coffee, your boss will ask you to do something that will last until the coffee is cold.

SANDILAND'S LAW:

Free time that unexpectedly becomes available will be wasted.

SCOTT'S LAW OF BUSINESS:

Never walk down a hallway in an office building without a piece of paper in your hand.

HARBOUR'S LAW:

The deadline is one week after the original deadline.

EDDIE'S LAW OF BUSINESS:

Never conduct negotiations before 10:00 A.M. or after 4:00 P.M. Before ten you appear too anxious, and after four they think you're desperate.

TABLE OF HANDY OFFICE EXCUSES:

1. That's the way we're always done it.

2. I didn't know you were in a hurry for it.

3. No one told me to go ahead.

4. I'm waiting for an OK.

5. How did I know this was different?

6. That's his job, not mine.

7. Wait t'il the boss comes back and ask her.

◥Tillis 的整理原則：

資料歸檔了，知道在哪的就永遠用不著。

資料如果未歸檔，要的時候就永遠找不到。

◥Owen 的秘書定律：

你才坐下來想喝杯熱咖啡，上司就找你做事情，等咖啡冷掉了才
放你走。

◥Sandiland 的定律：

意外的空閒一定會給糟蹋掉。

◥Scott 的公事定律：

在辦公大樓的走廊裡走動，千萬別兩手空空。

◥Harbour 的定律：

真正期限是原期限加一週。

◥Eddie 的公事定律：

早上十點前及下午四點後千萬別進行談判。十點前顯得你浮躁，
四點後人家認為你是狗急跳牆。

◥便利的辦公室藉口一覽表：

1. 大家都這樣做的。

2. 我不知道你急著要。

3. 沒人叫我動。

4. 我在等人家說可以。

5. 我怎麼知道這件不一樣。

6. 這是他的事，不是我的。

7. 等老闆回來再問老闆吧。

8. We don't make many mistakes.

9. I didn't think it was very important.

10. I'm so busy, I just can't get around to it.

11. I thought I told you.

12. I wasn't hired to do that.

◥DRUMMOND'S LAW OF PERSONNEL RECRUITING:

The ideal resume will turn up one day after the position is filled.

◥FOX ON YESMANSHIP:

It's worth scheming to be the bearer of good news.

Corollary: Don't be in the building when bad news arrives.

◥PINTO'S LAW:

Do someone a favor and it becomes your job.

◥CONNOR'S LAW:

If something is confidential, it will be left in the copier machine.

◥LANGSAM'S ORNITHOLOGICAL AXIOM:

It's difficult to soar with eagles when you work with turkeys.

8. 有時難免出錯。

9. 我以為不重要。

10. 我實在忙不過來。

11. 我不是跟你講過了嗎？

12. 人家可不是花錢雇我來做這個。

▼Drummond 的人員招募定律：
　人招募了，最合適者的履歷表才寄來。

▼Fox 論狗腿族：
　通報好消息，保證有甜頭。
　以此類推：壞消息來時別待在公司裡。

▼Pinto 的定律：
　幫人家的忙，結果變成你的事。

▼Connor 的定律：
　密字號的資料會被遺留在影印機裡。

▼Langsam 的鳥類學格言：
　跟火雞共事就很難與老鷹齊飛。

SYSTEMANTICS
系統學

*(from *Systemantics* by John Gall; Quandrangle/New York Times Book Co., 1977)

◥THE FUNDAMENTAL THEOREM:

New systems generate new problems.

◥Corollary:

Systems should not be unnecessarily multiplied.

◥THE GENERALIZED UNCERTAINTY PRINCIPLE:

Systems tend to grow, and as they grow, they encroach.
Alternative Formulations:

    1. Complicated systems produce unexpected outcomes.

    2. The total behavior of large systems cannot be predicted.

◥Corollary: The Non-Additivity Theorem of Systems-Behavior

A large system, produced by expanding the dimensions of a smaller system, does not behave like the smaller system.

◥THE FUNCTIONARY FALSITY:

People in systems do not do what the system says they are doing.

◥THE OPERATIONAL FALLACY:

The system itself does not do what it says it is doing.

◥FIRST LAW OF SYSTEMANTICS:

A complex system that works is invariably found to have evolved from a simple system that works.

◥SECOND LAW OF SYSTEMANTICS:

A complex system designey from scratch never works and cannot be patched up to make it work. You have to start over, beginning with a working simple system.

▼基本理則：
新系統產生新問題。

▼以此類推：
不需要增添的系統就別添。

▼普遍不穩定原則：
系統容易膨脹，膨脹了就會亂來。

類似說法：

　1. 複雜的系統製造料想不到的結果。

　2. 大系統的整體表現無法預測。

▼以此類推：系統行為的不可加定理
擴充小系統格局所得的大系統，其運作不會跟小系統類似。

▼功能假象：
系統說的是一套，其系統裡的人做的是另一套。

▼操作謬誤：
系統本身也是說一套做一套。

▼系統學第一定律：
有用的複雜系統無一不是發展自原來就有用的簡單系統。

▼系統學第二定律：
另起爐灶所設計的複雜系統從來就不能運作，怎麼補救也沒有用。一定要從頭做起，找個可用的簡單系統做基礎。

◥THE FUNDAMENTAL POSTULATES OF ADVANCED SYSTEMS THEORY:

1. Everything is a system.

2. Everything is part of a larger system.

3. The universe is infinitely systematized, both upward (larger systems) and downward (smaller systems).

4. All systems are infinitely complex. (The illusion of simplicity comes from focusing attention on one or a few variables.)

◥LE CHATELIER'S PRINCIPLE:

Complex systems tend to oppose their own proper function.

▼高級系統定理的基本前提：

　1. 一切事物都是系統。

　2. 一切事物都是大系統的一部分。

　3. 宇宙已經無限系統化，不管是往大處看，或者是往小處看。

　4. 所有系統都無限複雜。（會有簡單的假象，是因為只看少數幾個
　　　變數。）

▼Le Chatelier 的原則：

　複雜的系統會跟自己正常的功能作對。

SITUATIONAL
MURPHOLOGY
運氣篇

DRAZEN'S LAW OF RESTITUTION:

The time it takes to rectify a situation is inversely proportional to the time it took to do the damage.

Example: It takes longer to glue a vase together than to break one.

Example: It takes longer to lose x number of pounds than to gain x number of pounds.

ETORRE'S OBSERVATION:

The other line moves faster.

O'BRIEN'S VARIATION ON ETORRE'S OBSERVATION:

If you change lines, the one you just left will start to move faster than the one you are now in.

Kenton's Corollary:

Switching back screws up both lines and makes everybody angry.

THE QUEUE PRINCIPLE:

The longer you wait in line, the greater the likelihood that you are standing in the wrong line.

FLUGG'S RULE:

The slowest checker is always at the quick check-out lane.

VILE'S LAW OF ADVANCED LINESMANSHIP:

1. If you're running for a short line, it suddenly becomes a long line.
2. When you're waiting in a long line, the people behind you are shunted to a new, short line.
3. If you step out of a short line for a second, it becomes a long line.

▼Drazen 的賠償定律：

恢復的時間與破壞的時間成反比。

例子：黏合碎花瓶的時間就比打碎要久。

例子：減少 x 磅的肥肉花的時間比增加 x 磅的肥肉久。

▼Etorre 的觀察：

另一排隊伍動得更快。

▼O'Brien 變化 Etorre 的觀察：

如果你跳到別排去，原來那排就動得比你所在的那排快。

▼Kenton 類推：

如果又跳回來，就會把隊伍弄亂，把大家都惹火了。

▼排隊原則：

隊排得愈久，排錯行的可能愈大。

▼Flugg 的法則：

手腳最慢的檢查員，總是在快速通關窗口。

▼Vile 的進階排隊人定律：

1. 如果衝向短的那排，那排就忽然變長了。

2. 要是你排在長隊裡，你後面的人都會換到另一列短的去。

3. 短隊伍才離開一會，回來已經變長。

4. If you're in a short line, the people in front let in their friends and relatives and make it a long line.

5. A short line outside a building becomes a long line inside.

6. If you stand in one place long enough, you make a line.

HEID'S LAW OF LINES:

No matter how early you arrive, someone else is in line first.

LUPOSCHAINSKY'S HURRY-UP-AND-WAIT PRINCIPLE:

If you're early, it'll be cancelled.

If you knock yourself out to be on time, you'll have to wait.

If you're late, you'll be too late.

DEDERA'S LAW:

In a three-story building served by one elevator, nine times out of ten the elevator car will be on a floor where you are not.

GLUCK'S LAW:

Whichever way you turn upon entering an elevator, the buttons will be on the opposite side.

LYNCH'S LAW:

The elevator always comes after you have put down your bag.

WITTEN'S LAW:

Whenever you cut your fingernails you will find a need for them an hour later.

STORRY'S PRINCIPLE OF CRIMINAL INDICTMENT:

The degree of guilt is directly proportional to the intensity of the denial.

4. 如果你排的是短行，前頭的人就會讓親朋好友插隊，於是又變
   成長隊伍。

5. 門外的短隊伍在門內還有一長串。

6. 只要站著夠久，就有人跟你排成一列。

▼Heid 的行列定律：
不管你到得多早，已經有人在排。

▼Luposchainsky 的趕就得等定律：
早到就會取消。

盡可能準時就得等。

遲到就排不到。

▼Dedera 的定律：
在三樓的建築裡有一部電梯，這電梯九成不會在你所在的那層。

▼Gluck 的定律：
進電梯不管站哪邊，按紐總在另一邊。

▼Lynch 的定律：
把東西放下來等，電梯就來了。

▼Witten 的定律：
每次把指甲剪了，一小時後你就得用到指甲。

▼Storry 的定罪原則：
否認得愈激烈罪愈重。

▼ TRACY'S TIME OBSERVATION:

Good times end too quickly. Bad times go on forever.

▼ THIESSEN'S LAW OF ART:

The overwhelming prerequisite for the greatness of an artist is that artist's death.

▼ ELY'S LAW:

Wear the right costume and the part plays itself.

▼ FIRST RULE OF ACTING:

Whatever happens, look as if it was intended.

▼ ZADRA'S LAW OF BIOMECHANICS:

The severity of the itch is inversely proportional to the reach.

▼ THIESSEN'S LAW OF GASTRONOMY:

The hardness of the butter is in direct proportion to the softness of the roll.

▼ REVEREND CHICHESTER'S LAWS:

1. f the weather is extremely bad, church attendance will be down.
2. If the weather is extremely good, church attendance will be down.
3. If the bulletins are in short supply, church attendance will exceed all expectations.

▼ LAW OF BALANCE:

Bad habits will cancel out good ones.

Example: The orange juice and granola you had for breakfast will be canceled out by the cigarette you smoked on the way to work and the candy bar you just bought.

◥Tracy 的時間看法：
好日不長久，壞日恆久遠。

◥Thiessen 的藝術定律：
藝術家要偉大，有個絕對必要的先決條件，就是他得死掉。

◥Ely 的定律：
穿對戲服不用演也是戲。

◥演戲第一法則：
不管出了什麼差錯，讓觀眾覺得劇本就是這麼寫。

◥Zadra 的生物機械定律：
愈癢的就愈抓不到。

◥Thiessen 的美食定律：
奶油的硬度與麵包卷的軟度成正比。

◥Chichester 牧師的定律：
1. 天氣糟糕，到教堂的人會減少。
2. 風和日麗，到教堂的人會減少。
3. 如果剩沒幾張公告，到教堂的人數就會超乎預期。

◥平衡定律：
壞習慣會把好的抵消。
例子：早餐吃的柳橙汁和什錦果麥，就被你在
上班路上所抽的香菸與剛買的糖果塊抵
消。

CAFETERIA LAW:

The item you had your eye on the minute you walked in will be taken by the person in front of you.

DINER'S DILEMMA:

A clean tie attracts the soup of the day.

REYNOLD'S LAW OF CLIMATOLOGY:

Wind velocity increases directly with the cost of the hairdo.

JAN AND MARTHA'S LAW OF THE BEAUTY SHOP:

The most flattering comments on your hair come the day before you're scheduled to have it cut.

JILLY'S LAW:

The worse the haircut, the slower it grows out.

HUTCHINSON'S LAW:

If a situation requires undivided attention, it will occur simultaneously with a compelling distraction.

FULLER'S LAW OF JOURNALISM:

The farther away the disaster or accident occurs, the greater the number of dead and injured required for it to become a story.

LAWS OF TRUTH IN REPORTING:

1. The closer you are to the facts of a situation, the more obvious are the errors in the news coverage.
2. The farther you are from the facts of a situation, the more you tend to believe the news coverage.

WEATHERWAX'S POSTULATE:

The degree to which you overreact to information will be in inverse proportion to its accuracy.

▼自助餐定律：

你看準的一道菜，等走到了就被前面那個人拿走。

▼用餐者的難題：

今日湯最愛剛洗的領帶。

▼Reynold 的氣象學定律：

風速與髮型的造價成正比。

▼Jan 和 Martha 的美容院定律：

你打算剪頭髮的前一天，才會有人用最好聽的話誇讚你的頭髮。

▼Jilly 的定律：

頭髮剪得愈失敗，長得愈慢。

▼Hutchinson 的定律：

如果哪件事要求全神貫注，就會跟某件非讓你分神不可的事一起發生。

▼Fuller 的新聞定律：

災難或意外的發生地點愈遙遠、死傷人數愈多，就愈值得報導。

▼報導的真象定律：

1. 離事件發生地點愈近，新聞內容的錯誤愈明顯。
2. 離事件發生地愈遠，愈容易相信報導的內容。

▼Weatherwax 的假設：

你對某個消息過度反應的程度，與其精確度成反比。

◥DAVIS' LAW:

If a headline ends in a question mark, the answer is "no."

◥WEAVER'S LAW:

When several reporters share a cab on an assignment, the reporter in the front seat pays for all.

◥Doyle's Corollary:

No matter how many reporters share a cab, and no matter who pays, each puts the full fare on his or her own expense account.

◥THE LAW OF THE LETTER:

The best way to inspire fresh thoughts is to seal the letter.

◥HOWDEN'S LAW:

You remember to mail a letter only when you're nowhere near a mailbox.

◥LAWS OF POSTAL DELIVERY:

1. Love letters, business contracts, and money you are due always arrive three weeks late.
2. Junk mail arrives the day it was sent.

◥JONES' LAW OF ZOOS AND MUSEUMS:

The most interesting specimen will not be labeled.

◥LAW OF CHRISTMAS DECORATING:

The outdoor lights that tested perfectly develop burn-outs as soon as they are strung on the house.

◥MILSTEAD'S CHRISTMAS CARD RULE:

After you have mailed your last card, you will receive a card from someone you overlooked.

▼Davis 的定律：
標題以問號作結的，答案就是否定。

▼Weaver 的定律：
幾個記者共乘一輛計程車跑新聞，坐在前座的得付所有人的車資。

▼Doyle 的類推：
不管多少個記者共乘一輛計程車，也不管是誰付車費，每個人在出差費用欄裡都會填上全部的車費。

▼信件定律：
激發新想法的最佳方法就是把信封封上。

▼Howden 的定律：
在沒有郵筒的地方，才會想起有信要寄。

▼郵件傳遞定律：
1. 情書、生意合約、該收到的錢等，總是慢三週。
2. 垃圾信件寄出當天就到了。

▼Jones 的動物園和博物館定律：
最有趣的展覽品就是沒有說明標籤。

▼耶誕裝飾定律：
屋外燈飾試的時候沒問題，一掛到屋裡就壞了好幾個。

▼Milstead 的耶誕卡法則：
寄出最後一張卡片後，就會收到你漏掉的人寄來的賀卡。

JONES' LAW OF PUBLISHING:

Some errors will always go unnoticed until the book is in print.

Bloch's Corollary:

The first page the author turns to upon receiving an advance copy will be the page containing the worst error.

PHOTOGRAPHER'S LAWS:

1. The best shots happen immediately after the last frame is exposed.
2. The other best shots are generally attempted through the lens cap.
3. Any surviving best shots are ruined when someone inadvertently opens the darkroom door and all of the dark leaks out.

DOWLING'S LAW OF PHOTOGRAPHY:

One missed photographic opportunity creates a desire to purchase two additional pieces of equipment.

SIR WALTER'S LAW:

The tendency of smoke from a cigarette, barbecue or campfire to drift into a person'S face varies directly with that person't sensitivity to smoke.

KAUFFMAN'S LAW OF AIRPORTS:

The distance to the gate is inversely proportional to the time available to catch your flight.

ROGERS' LAW:

As soon as the coffee is served, the airliner encounters turbulence.

▼Jones 的出版法則：
　有些錯誤要到書出版了才會出現。

▼Bloch 類推：
　作者收到再校本，一翻開就會看到最離譜的錯誤。

▼攝影師定律：
　1. 拍一卷底片剛完，絕佳的鏡頭就出現。
　2. 拍其他絕佳鏡頭的時候，鏡頭蓋通常沒取下。
　3. 僅存的絕佳鏡頭在沖片時，會有個冒失鬼打開暗房的門，讓一切都曝光。

▼Dowling 的攝影定律：
　錯過一個好鏡頭，就會激起多買兩個配件的慾望。

▼Walter 爵士的定律：
　不管來自香菸、烤肉、營火的煙，衝著人飄去的機率與這個人對煙的敏感程度成正比。

▼Kauffman 的機場定律：
　到登機口的距離，與趕飛機所需的時間成反比。

▼Rogers 的定律：
　咖啡才來，飛機就遇上亂流。

◥Davis' Explanation of Rogers' Law:

Serving coffee on an aircraft causes turbulence.

◥BASIC BAGGAGE PRINCIPLE:

Whatever carousel you stand by, your baggage will come in on another one.

◥ANGUS' EXCHANGE AXIOM:

When traveling overseas, the exchange rate improves markedly the day after one has purchased foreign currency.

Corollary: Upon returning home, the rate drops again as soon as one has converted all unused foreign currency.

◥CROSBY'S LAW:

You can tell how bad a musical is by how many times the chorus yells, "Hooray!"

◥BYRNE'S LAW OF CONCRETING:

When you pour, it rains.

◥McLAUGHLIN'S LAW:

In a key position in every genealogy you will find a John Smith from London.

◥WRIGHT'S LAW:

A doctor can bury his or her mistakes, but an architect can only advise the client to plant vines.

◥RUSH'S RULE OF GRAVITY:

When you drop change at a vending machine, the pennies will fall nearby while the other coins will roll out of sight.

▼Davis 解釋 Rogers 的定律：
飛機上供應咖啡會製造亂流。

▼基本行李原則：
不管站在哪條行李輸送帶前，你的行李就是會在別條輸送帶上出
現。

▼Angus 的匯率格言：
到海外旅行，買了外匯的隔天匯率就漲了。
以此類推：回國才把沒用完的外匯全賣掉後，匯率又降了。

▼Crosby 的定律：
音樂片裡，合聲小組吆喝的次數愈多，該片愈爛。

▼Byrne 的混凝土鋪路定律：
混凝土一鋪就下雨。

▼McLaughlin 的定律：
不管哪本族譜，都有一位倫敦來的 John Smith 位在重要的位置。

▼Wright 的定律：
醫生可以埋葬自己的錯誤，建築師只能建議人家種些藤蔓。

▼Rush 的萬有引力定律：
在販賣機前要是掉硬幣，一元的會掉在腳邊，
五元、十元就不知道滾到哪去。

SOCIOMURPHOLOGY
(HUMANSHIP)
交際篇

◥ SHIRLEY'S LAW:

Most people deserve each other.

◥ HARRIS' LAMENT:

All the good ones are taken.

◥ ARTHUR'S LAWS OF LOVE:

1. People to whom you are attracted invariably think you remind them of someone else.
2. The love letter you finally got the courage to send will be delayed in the mail long enough for you to make a fool of yourself in person.
3. Other people's romantic gestures seem novel and exciting. Your own romantic gestures seem foolish and clumsy.

◥ LAW OF HUMAN QUIRKS:

Everyone wants to be noticed, but no one wants to be stared at.

◥ ANDERSON'S AXIOM:

You can only be young once, but you can be immature forever.

◥ BEDFELLOW'S RULE:

The one who snores will fall asleep first.

◥ THOMS' LAW OF MARITAL BLISS:

The length of a marriage is inversely proportional to the amount spent on the wedding.

◥ MURPHY'S FIRST LAW FOR HUSBANDS:

The first time you go out after your wife's birthday you will see the gift you gave her marked down 50 percent.

▼Shirley 的定律：
　人際關係大半是半斤配八兩。

▼Harris 的悲哀：
　條件好的人都有伴了。

▼Arthur 的愛的定律：
　1. 吸引你的人，個個都覺得你讓他想起某人。
　2. 你終於有勇氣寫情書，信卻在郵寄途中耽擱許久，讓你得親自
　　　跑去出糗。
　3. 別人的示愛方式既新鮮又刺激，自己的就既笨又拙。

▼怪癖定律：
　大家都希望受人矚目，卻沒有人喜歡給人盯著看。

▼Anderson 的格言：
　人只能年輕一次，但可以永遠幼稚。

▼床頭定律：
　打鼾的人總是先睡著的那個。

▼Thoms 的婚姻幸福定律：
　婚姻維持的時間，與婚禮的花費成反比。

▼莫非給丈夫的第一條定律：
　老婆生日後第一次出門，你就會看到送她的禮
　物已經變半價。

◥Corollary:

If she is with you, she will assume you chose it because it was cheap.

◥MURPHY'S SECOND LAW FOR HUSBANDS:

The gifts you buy your wife are never as apropos as the gifts your neighbor buys his wife.

◥MURPHY'S THIRD LAW FOR HUSBANDS:

Your wife's stored possessions will be on top of your stored possessions.

◥MURPHY'S FIRST LAW FOR WIVES:

If you ask your husband to pick up five items at the supermarket and then add one more as an afterthought, he'll forget two of the first five.

◥MURPHY'S SECOND LAW FOR WIVES:

The snapshots you take of your husband are always more flattering than the ones he takes of you.

◥MURPHY'S THIRD LAW FOR WIVES:

Whatever arrangements you make for the division of household duties, your husband's job will be easier.

◥GILLENSON'S (de-sexed) LAWS OF EXPECTATION:

1. Never get excited about a blind date because of how he or she sounds over the phone.
2. Never get excited about a person because of what he or she looks like from behind.

◥COLVARD'S LOGICAL PREMISES:

All probabilities are 50 percent. Either a thing will happen or it won't.

▼以此類推：
如果她在身邊，心裡就會認為你是因為便宜才選這個禮物。

▼莫非給丈夫的第二條定律：
你送老婆的禮物，永遠比不上鄰居送他老婆的禮物來得合宜。

▼莫非給丈夫的第三條定律：
儲藏室裡，老婆的東西一定壓在你的上頭。

▼莫非給太太的第一條定律：
你要老公到超級市場買五樣東西，後來你又想到一樣告訴他，他保證會把前五項裡的兩樣忘掉。

▼莫非給太太的第二條定律：
你幫老公照的相一定照美了，他幫你照卻照醜了。

▼莫非給太太的第三條定律：
不管家事怎麼分，老公分到的一定比較簡單。

▼Gillenson 的（與性無關的）期望定律：
1. 盲目約會的對象，不管電話裡聲音多美都別高興得太早。
2. 不管對象從背後看多美，都別高興得太早。

▼Colvard 的邏輯的前提：
所有的機率都是百分之五十，不管會不會發生。

◣ Colvard's Unconscionable Commentary:

This is especially true when dealing with women.

◣ Grelb's Commentary on Colvard's Premise:

Likelihoods, however, are 90 percent against you.

◣ CHEIT'S LAMENT:

If you help a friend in need, he is sure to remember you—the next time he is in need.

◣ FARMER'S CREDO:

Sow your wild oats on Saturday night—then on Sunday pray for crop failure.

◣ ESQUIRE'S COMMENT:

The better the relationship starts out, the faster it fades.

◣ RUBY'S PRINCIPLE OF CLOSE ENCOUNTERS:

The probability of meeting someone you know increases when you are with someone you don't want to be seen with.

◣ JOHNSON'S LAW:

If, in the course of several months, only three worthwhile social events take place, they will all fall on the same evening.

◣ DENNISTON'S LAW:

Virtue is its own punishment.

◣ Denniston's Corollary:

If you do something right once, someone will ask you to do it again.

▼Colvard 的沒良心補充：
跟女人打交道便是如此。

▼Grelb 評 Colvard 的邏輯的前提：
不過對你不利的總是九成。

▼Cheit 的悲哀：
雪中送炭人家一定不會忘記──下次下雪沒炭又會想起你。

▼Farmer 的信條：
週六晚上隨便播種，到週日就祈禱可別有收成。

▼Esquire 的評語：
開始愈親，散得愈快。

▼Ruby 的冤家路窄原則：
你不想見到某人，跟此人相遇的機會就增加。

▼Johnson 的定律：
如果幾個月裡只有三場值得參加的社交活動，那麼一定排在同一個晚上。

▼Denniston 的定律：
美德本身就是一種報應。

▼Denniston 以此類推：
如果你做了什麼好事，別人就要你再做一次。

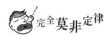

▼Bloch's Commentary:

Denniston't Corollary applies to the statement: "Virtuous action will never go unpunished." Denniston't Law has broader implications.

▼MASON'S LAW OF SYNERGISM:

The one day you'd sell your soul for something, souls are a glut.

▼RON'S OBSERVATIONS FOR TEENAGERS:

1. The pimples don't appear until the hour before the date.

2. The scratch on the CD is always through the song you like most.

▼JOHNSON AND LAIRD'S LAW:

A toothache tends to start on Saturday night.

▼SCHRIMPTON'S LAW OF TEENAGE OPPORTUNITY:

When opportunity knocks, you're got headphones on.

▼Bloch 的評語：

　　Denniston 的類推可以用到下面這句話：「好心不會沒有報應。」
　　不過 Denniston 的定律含義更多。

▼Mason 的共同作用定律：

　　哪天你想出賣靈魂，靈魂就供過於求。

▼Ron 給青少年的心得：

　　1. 青春痘要在約會前一個鐘頭才會冒出來。
　　2. CD 上的擦痕一定劃過你最愛聽的歌。

▼Johnson 和 Laird 的定律：

　　牙痛通常週六晚上來。

▼Schrimpton 的青少年機會定律：

　　機會來敲門，兩耳卻塞著耳機。

▼UNDERLYING PRINCIPLE OF SOCIO-GENETICS:

Superiority is recessive.

▼PROFESSOR BLOCK'S MOTTO:

Forgive and remember.

▼JACOB'S LAW:

To err is human—to blame it on someone else is even more human.

▼EDELSTEIN'S ADVICE:

Don't worry over what other people are thinking about you. They're too busy worrying over what you are thinking about them.

▼MEADER'S LAW:

Whatever happens to you, it will previously have happened to everyone you know.

▼BOCKLAGE'S LAW:

He who laughs last—probably didn't get the joke.

▼FIRST LAW OF SOCIO-GENETICS:

Celibacy is not hereditary.

▼FARBER'S LAW:

Necessity is the mother of strange bedfellows.

▼HARTLEY'S LAW:

Never sleep with anyone crazier than yourself.

▼BECKHAP'S LAW:

Beauty times brains equals a constant.

▼PARKER'S LAW:

Beauty is only skin deep, but ugly goes clean to the bone.

社會遺傳學的內在原則：
一代總是不如一代。

Block 教授的座右銘：
饒人但記恨。

Jacob 的定律：
犯錯本屬人性——把錯怪到別人身上更合乎人性。

Edelstein 的建議：
不必擔心別人對你會有什麼想法。別人忙著擔心你對他們會有什麼想法都來不及了。

Meader 的定律：
不管你遇到什麼事，你認識的人全都經歷過了。

Bocklage 的定律：
最後笑的人——大概是沒聽懂笑話。

社會遺傳學第一定律：
單身貴族不會遺傳。

Farber 的定律：
有需求，才會有不搭軋的床邊伴侶。

Hartley 的定律：
別跟比自己更瘋的人同床。

Beckhap 的定律：
美貌乘上腦筋等於常數。

Parker 的定律：
美麗只是皮相，不過醜陋卻是醜到骨子裡頭去。

 完全莫非定律

PARDO'S POSTULATES:

1. Anything good in life is either illegal, immoral, or fattening.
2. The three faithful things in life are money, a dog, and an old woman.
3. Don't care if you're rich or not, as long as you can live comfortably and have everything you want.

STEINKOPFF'S EXTENSION TO PARDO'S FIRST POSTULATE:

The good thing in life also cause cancer in laboratory mice and are taxed beyond reality.

CAPTAIN PENNY'S LAW:

You can fool all of the people some of the time, and some of the people all of the time, but you can't fool Mom.

ISSAWI'S LAW OF THE CONSERVATION OF EVIL:

The total amount of evil in any system remains constant. Hence, any diminution in one direction—for instance, a reduction in poverty or unemployment—is accompanied by an increase in another, e.g., crime or air pollution.

KATZ'S LAW:

Men and nations will act rationally when all other possibilities have been exhausted.

PARKER'S LAW OF POLITICAL STATEMENTS:

The truth of any proposition has nothing to do with its credibility and vice versa.

MR. COLE'S AXIOM:

The sum of the intelligence on the planet remains a constant; the population, however, continues to grow.

▼Pardo 的心得：

1. 人生裡美好的事物通常不是不合法、不道德，就是會使人發胖。

2. 人生裡有三樣東西忠心不二：錢、狗、老女人。

3. 只要能過得舒舒服服、要什麼有什麼，不必在乎自己是富是窮。

▼Steinkopff 的引申 Pardo 的心得：

人生裡美好的事物還會讓實驗室的老鼠致癌，稅也重得離譜。

▼Penny 船長的定律：

你有辦法騙了大家一時，或騙幾個人一世，但你騙不了你媽。

▼Issawi 的壞處不滅定律：

所有系統裡的壞處總有一定的量。因此一方面改善了，像是減少貧窮與失業率，另一方面的就會增加，像是犯罪率與空氣汙染。

▼Katz 的定律：

人與國家會依理性行事——等別的辦法都試完了以後。

▼Parker 的政治言論定律：

任何提議是否有道理，與聽來有沒有道理無關，反之亦然。

▼Cole 先生的格言：

地球上的智力總和是個定數；不過人口持續增加。

◥LAW OF THE INDIVIDUAL:

Nobody really cares or understands what anyone else is doing.

◥STEELE'S PLAGIARISM OF SOMEBODY'S PHILOSOPHY:

Everybody should believe in something—I believe I'll have another drink.

◥McCLAUGHRY'S CODICIL TO JONES' MOTTO:

To make an enemy, do someone a favor.

◥CANADA BILL JONES' MOTTO:

It's morally wrong to allow suckers to keep their money.

◥Supplement:

A Smith and Wesson beats four aces.

◥LEVY'S LAW:

That segment of the community with which one has the greatest sympathy as a liberal inevitably turns out to be one of the most narrow-minded and bigoted segments of the community.

◥Kelly's Reformation:

Nice guys don't finish nice.

◥THE KENNEDY CONSTANT:

Don't get mad—get even.

◥JONES' MOTTO:

Friends come and go, but enemies accumulate.

◥VIQUE'S LAW:

A man without religion is like a fish without a bicycle.

▼個人定律：
　誰也沒有真正關心或者了解別人做的事。

▼Steele 抄來的人生哲學：
　人總要有堅持──我堅持再來一杯。

▼McClaughry 補 Jones 的座右銘：
　想樹立敵人就幫人一個忙。

▼加拿大 Bill Jones 的座右銘：
　傻子有錢是件不道德的事。

▼補充：
　某位 Smith 和 Wesson 打敗四張 A。

▼Levy 的定律：
　社群中最有同情心的開明人士，不可避免會成為社群中最心胸狹
　窄且固執己見的一群。

▼Kelly 的改寫：
　好人會變壞。

▼Kennedy 常理：
　生氣無用，要以牙還牙。

▼Jones 的座右銘：
　朋友有來有去，敵人只增不減。

▼Vique 的定律：
　人沒有宗教，就像魚沒有腳踏車。

◤THE FIFTH RULE:

You have taken yourself too seriously.

◤SARTRE'S OBSERVATION:

Hell is others.

◤DOOLEY'S LAW:

Trust everybody, but cut the cards.

◤ZAPPA'S LAW:

There art two things on earth that are universal: hydrogen and stupidity.

◤MUNDER'S THEOREM:

For every "10" there are ten "1s."

◤DYKSTRA'S LAW:

Everybody is somebody else's weirdo.

◤MEYERS' LAW:

In a social situation, that which is most difficult to do is usually the right thing to do.

第五法則：
你把自己想得太偉大。

沙特（法國哲學家）的心得：
他人即地獄。

Dooley 的定律：
相信別人，不過牌還是要切。

Zappa 的定律：
地球上有兩件事無所不在：氫氣與傻氣。

Munder 的理則：
每個十都是十個一。

Dykstra 的定律：
一物厭一物。

Meyers 的定律：
現實社會裡，最難做的通常就是正當的做法。

YOUNG'S PRINCIPLE OF EMERGENT INDIVIDUATION:

Everyone wants to peel his own banana.

COHEN'S LAW:

People are divided into two groups—the righteous and the unrighteous—and the righteous do the dividing.

THE IRE PRINCIPLE:

Never try to pacify people at the height of their rage.

PYTHON'S PRINCIPLE OF TV MORALITY:

There is nothing wrong with sex on television, just as long as you don't fall off.

KENT FAMILY LAW:

Never change your plans because of the weather.

LIVINGSTON'S LAWS OF FAT:

1. Fat expands to fill any apparel worn.

2. A fat person walks in the middle of the hall.

Corollary: Two fat people will walk side by side, whether they know each other or not.

LAW OF ARRIVAL:

Those who live closest arrive latest.

THE THREE LEAST CREDIBLE SENTENCES IN THE ENGLISH LANGUAGE:

1."The check is in the mail."

2."Of course I'll respect you in the morning."

3."I'm from the government and I'm here to help you."

▼Young 的自然個性化原則：
自己的香蕉大家都想自己剝。

▼Cohen 的定律：
人分兩種，正直與不正直——這是正直人的分法。

▼Ire 原則：
人家正在氣頭上就別去安撫。

▼Python 的電視道德原則：
電視上有床戲沒什麼不對，只要你不因此跌倒的話。

▼Kent 家庭定律：
別看天氣改變計畫。

▼Livingston 的肥胖定律：
1. 不管穿什麼衣服，肥肉都能撐滿。
2. 胖子過大廳都走中央。
以此類推：兩個胖子一定並肩而行，不管彼此認不認識。

▼到達定律：
住的最近，到的最晚。

▼英文裡頭，三句最不可信的話：

1.「支票已經寄出。」
2.「明天早上我還是會敬重你。」
3.「我是政府派來協助你的。」

MEDICAL MURPHOLOGY
醫學篇

SIX PRINCIPLES FOR PATIENTS:

1. Just because your doctor has a name for your condition doesn't mean your doctor knows what it is.

2. The more boring and out-of-date the magazines in the waiting room, the longer you will have to wait for your scheduled appointment.

3. Only adults have difficulty with childproof bottles.

4. You never have the right number of pills left on the last day of a prescription.

5. The pills to be taken with meals will be the least appetizing ones.

   Corollary: Even water tastes bad when taken on doctor's orders.

6. If your condition seems to be getting better, it's probably your doctor getting sick.

PARKINSON'S LAW FOR MEDICAL RESEARCH:

Successful research attracts the bigger grant, which makes further research impossible.

MATZ'S WARNING:

Beware of the physician who is great at getting out of trouble.

MATZ'S RULE REGARDING MEDICATIONS:

A drug is that substance which, when injected into a rat, will produce a scientific report.

COCHRANE'S APHORISM:

Before ordering a test, decide what you will do if it is 1)positive, or 2)negative. If both answers are the same, don't do the test.

▼病人原則六條：

1. 醫生說得出病情的名字，並不表示他知道是什麼病。

2. 等候室裡的雜誌愈是無聊過時，要等到你的號碼就愈久。

3. 只有大人打不開防兒童打開的瓶子。

4. 最後一天的那份藥，藥丸數目一定不對。

5. 和正餐一起吃的藥一定最難吃。

以此類推：要是醫生叮嚀多喝水，連水都難喝。

6. 如果你的病好轉，八成是醫生病了。

▼Parkinson 的醫學研究定律：

研究愈成功，專利權就愈久，於是就更不可能做進一步的研究。

▼Matz 的警告：

要當心擅於脫困的醫生。

▼Matz 的醫療法則：

藥物這種東西，注入老鼠體內便會產生科學報告。

▼Cochrane 的雋語：

進行測試之前，先決定若陽性反應要如何、陰
性反應要如何。如果兩者相同，就別測試了。

EDDS' LAW OF RADIOLOGY:

The colder the X-ray table, the more of your body you are required to place on it.

BERNSTEIN'S PRECEPT:

The radiologists' national flower is the hedge.

LORD COHEN'S COMMENT:

The feasibility of an operation is not the best indication for its performance.

TELESCO'S LAWS OF NURSING:

1. All the IVs are at the other end of the hall.
2. A physician's ability is inversely proportional to his or her availability.
3. There are two kinds of adhesive tape: that which won't stay on and that which won't come off.
4. Everybody wants a pain shot at the same time.
5. Everybody who didn't want a pain shot when you were passing out pain shots wants one when you are passing out sleeping pills.

BARACH'S RULE:

An alcoholic is a person who drinks more than his own physician.

▼Edds 的放射線學定律：
　　Ｘ光照射枱愈冷，醫生要你躺上去的身體面積就愈大。

▼Bernstein 的格言：
　　放射線學家的國花是樹籬。

▼Cohen 爵士的評語：
　　手術的難易程度，不能做為是否動手術的依據。

▼Telesco 的看護定律：
　　1. 靜派注射室一定在大廳另一邊。
　　2. 醫生的醫術與有空的時間成反比。
　　3. 膠布有兩種：一種貼不住，一種撕不下。
　　4. 要打止痛針的人會一起來。
　　5. 你來打止痛針的時候沒人要打；你來發安眠藥時，大家都要止痛針。

▼Barach 的法則：
　　酒鬼就是酒喝得比自己的醫生多的人。

SPORTSMANSHIP-MANSHIP

運動與娛樂篇

◥WISE FAN'S LAMENT:

Fools rush in—and get the best seats.

◥BREDA'S RULE:

At any event, the people whose seats are farthest from the aisle arrive last.

◥MOSER'S LAW OF SPECTATOR SPORTS:

Exciting plays occur only while you are watching the scoreboard or out buying a hot dog.

◥BOB'S LAW OF TELEVISED SPORTS:

If you switch from one football game to another in order to avoid a commercial, the second game will be running a commercial too.

◥MURRAY'S RULES OF THE ARENA:

1. Nothing is ever so bad it can't be made worse by firing the coash.
2. The wrong quarterback is the one that's in there.
3. A free agent is anything but.
4. Hockey is a game played by six good players and the home team.
5. Whatever can go to New York will.

◥INDISPUTABLE LAW OF SPORTS CONTRACTS:

The more money the free agent signs for, the less effective he is the following season.

◥KNOX'S PRINCIPLE OF STAR QUALITY:

Whenever a superstar is traded to your favorite team, he fades. Whenever your team trades away a useless no-name, he immediately rises to stardom.

◤聰明球迷的悲哀：

傻子一衝進來，把好位子搶走了。

◤Breda 的法則：

不管是什麼比賽，坐最裡頭的人最晚到。

◤Moser 的觀賽定律：

有精采演出時，你正好在看計分表，要不然就是出去買熱狗。

◤Bob 的轉播比賽定律：

甲頻道的足球賽進廣告，你轉到乙頻道的足球賽，那邊正好也會進廣告。

◤Murray 的運動場法則：

1.就算情況糟透了，把教練開除會更糟。

2.派上場的四分衛一定有問題。

3.自由經紀人從來就不是免費的。（free 同時指「自由」與「免費」。）

4.曲棍球這種球賽是由六名好球員與地主隊比賽的球賽。

5.能去紐約的都去了。

◤無可爭論之運動員合約定律：

自由經紀人簽約金愈多，下一季他就愈沒用。

◤Knox 的明星特質原則：

運動巨星轉到你心愛的球隊就凋零。無名小卒一離開你心愛的球隊就聲譽日隆。

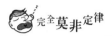

HERTZBERG'S LAW OF WING WALKING:

Never leave hold of what you've got until you've got hold of something clse.

TERMAN'S LAW OF INNOVATION:

If you want a track team to win the high jump, you find one person who ean jump seven feet, not seven people who can jump one foot.

LAVIA'S LAW OF TENNIS:

A mediocre player will sink to the level of his opposition.

LEFTY GOMEZ'S LAW:

If you don't throw it, they can't hit it.

LAW OF PRACTICE:

Plays that work in theory do not work in practice.

Plays that work in practice do not work during the game.

▼Hertzberg 的 wing walking 定律：
　一樣東西拿穩了，才可以放掉手上擁有的東西。

▼Terman 的革新定律：
　如果徑賽隊伍想贏得跳高比賽，要的是一個能跳七呎的人，而不
　是七個能跳一呎的人。

▼Lavia 的網球定律：
　二流選手會降到與對手的水準相當。

▼Lefty Gomez 的定律：
　如果你不投球，對方就打不到。

▼練習定律：
　理論上行得通的動作，練習就做不到。
　練習時做得出來的動作，比賽時就使不出來。

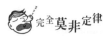

SIGSTAD'S LAW:

When it gets to be your trun, they change the rules.

THE POKER PRINCIPLE:

Never do card tricks for the group you play poker with.

STENDERUP'S LAW:

The sooner you fall behind, the more time you will have to catch up.

WAGNER'S LAW OF SPORTS COVERAGE:

When the camera isolates on a male athlete, he will spit, pick or scratch.

DEAL'S LAW OF SAILING:

1. The amount of wind will vary inversely with the number and experience of the people you take on board.
2. No matter how strong the breeze when you leave the dock, once you have reached the farthest point from the port, the wind will die.

DORR'S LAW OF ATHLETICS:

In an otherwise empty locker room, any two individuals will have adjoining lockers.

THE RULE OF THE RALLY:

The only way to make up for being lost is to make record time while you are lost.

PORKINGHAM'S LAWS OF SPORTFISHING:

1. The time available to go fishing shrinks as the fishing season draws nearer.

▼Sigstad 的定律：
　輪到你的時候，人家改變規則了。

▼撲克牌定律：
　別在牌友面前表演牌戲。

▼Stenderup 的定律：
　落後得愈早，趕上就愈花時間。

▼Wagner 的運動攝影定律：
　給男運動員來個特寫時，他正好在吐口水、挖鼻子、抓癢。

▼Deal 的帆船運動定律：
　1.風的量與船上同伴的經驗與人數成反比。
　2.不管離開碼頭時風力多麼充足，等你開到離港口最遠的一點，風
　　就停了。

▼Dorr 的運動定律：
　儲物櫃要不就是沒人用，要不就是兩個在用的人得緊緊挨著。

▼公路賽車定律：
　迷路時唯一的補救之道，就是創造耗時最長的紀錄。

▼Porkingham 的釣魚定律：
　1.有空釣魚的時間隨著釣魚季節接近而減少。

2. The least experienced fisherman always catches the biggest fish.

Corollary: The more elaborate and costly the equipment, the greater the chance of having to stop at the fish market on the way home.

3. The worse your line is tangled, the better the fishing is around you.

◤MICHEHL'S RULE FOR PROSPECTIVE MOUNTAIN CLIMBERS:

The mountain gets steeper as you get closer.

◤Frothingham's Corollary:

The mountain looks closer than it is.

◤SHEDENHELM'S LAW OF BACKPACKING:

All trails have more uphill sections than they have level or downhill sections.

◤LAW OF BRIDGE:

It's always the partner's fault.

◤SMITH'S LAWS OF BRIDGE:

1. If your hand contains a singleton or a void, that is the suit your partner will bid.

2. If your hand contains the King, Jack, 9 of diamonds and the Ace of spades, when the dummy is spread to your left it will contain the Ace, Queen, 10 of diamonds and the King of spades.

3. The trump suit never breaks favorably when you are the declarer.

2.最菜的釣手總是釣到最大的魚。

以此類推：裝備愈複雜、愈昂貴，回家的路上愈有可能上魚市
場。

3.釣魚線纏得愈亂，身邊就有愈大的魚。

▼Michehl 的明日登山專家定律：
山靠愈近就愈陡。

▼Frothingham 類推：
山看起來總是近。

▼Shedenhelm 的背包遠足定律：
山路的上坡路永遠比平路或下坡路多。

▼橋牌定律：
錯永遠出在伙伴身上。

▼Smith 的橋牌定律：
1.如果手上哪個花色只有一張或者沒半張，對家就會叫那個花
色。

2.如果你手上有紅磚 K、J、9 和黑桃 A，而夢家在你左手邊時，
他就有紅磚 A、Q、10 和黑桃 K。

3.你是莊家時，夢家攤出的王牌總是你的弱門。

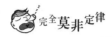

THOMAS' LAW:

The one who least wants to play is the one who will win.

HENRY'S QUIRK OF HUMAN NATURE:

Nobody loves a winner who wins all the time.

TODD'S LAW:

All things being equal, you lose.

Corollary: All things being in your favor, you still lose.

JENSEN'S LAW:

Win or lose, you lose.

▼Thomas 的定律：
　最不想玩牌的人總是贏。

▼Henry 的人類怪癖論：
　常勝軍總是沒人愛。

▼Todd 的定律：
　實力相當時你會輸。
　以此類推：形勢對你有利時，你還是輸。

▼Jensen 的定律：
　不管輸贏，你都是輸家。

ROADSMANSHIP
出外篇

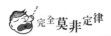 完全莫非定律

OLIVER'S LAW OF LOCATION:

No matter where you go, there you are!

FIRST LAW OF TRAVEL:

It always takes longer to get there than to get back.

THE AIRPLANE LAW:

When the plane you are on is late, the plane you want to transfer to is on time.

LAW OF PROMOTIONAL TOURS:

Jet lag accumulates unidirectionally toward maximum difficulty to perform.

STITZER'S VACATION PRINCIPLE:

When packing for a vacation, take half as much clothing and twice as much money.

SNIDER'S LAW:

Nothing can be done in one trip.

LAW OF BICYCLING:

No matter which way you ride, it's uphill and against the wind.

HUMPHRIES' LAW OF BICYCLING:

The shortest route has the steepest hills.

KELLY'S LAW OF AERIAL NAVIGATION:

The most important information on any chart is on the fold.

GRANDPA CHARNOCK'S LAW:

You never really learn to swear until you learn to drive.

▼Oliver 的地點定律：
　到了就好，管他到哪。

▼第一條旅行定律：
　去的時間總是比回程多。

▼飛機定律：
　如果你坐的這班飛機誤點了，要轉的那班飛機就準時。

▼促銷旅行定律：
　時差無一不是以最大量累積，讓你累得不能動。

▼Stitzer 的假期原則：
　為旅行打包時，衣服少帶一半，錢多帶一倍。

▼Snider 的定律：
　光跑一趟總是辦不成事。

▼腳踏車定律：
　不管哪條路，一定是上坡而逆風。

▼Humphries 的腳踏車定律：
　最短的路最陡。

▼Kelly 的航空定律：
　任何表上最重要的資訊都在對折處。

▼Charnock 老公公的定律：
　會開車你才真的學得會罵髒話。

◥ VILE'S LAW OF ROADSMANSHIP:

Your own car uses more gas and oil than anyone else's.

◥ GRELB'S REMINDER:

Eighty percent of all people consider themselves to be above-average drivers.

◥ PHILLIPS' LAW:

Four-wheel drive just means getting stuck in more inaccessible places.

◥ LAW OF LIFE'S HIGHWAY:

If everything is coming your way, you're in the wrong lane.

◥ RELATIVITY FOR CHILDREN:

Time moves slower in a fast-moving vehicle.

◥ ATHENA'S RULES OF DRIVING COURTESY:

If you allow someone to get in front of you, either:

a. the car in front will be the last one over a railroad crossing, and you will be stuck waiting for a long, slow-moving train; or

b. you both will have the same destination, and the other car will get the last parking space.

◥ LEMAR'S PARKING POSTULATE:

If you have to park six blocks away, you will find two new parking spaces right in front of the building entrance.

◥ KARINTHY'S DEFINITION:

A bus is a vehicle that goes on the other side in the opposite direction.

▼Vile 的上路定律：

你的車耗油比誰都兇。

▼Grelb 的提醒：

百分之八十的人都認為自己是中上程度的駕駛。

▼Phillips 的定律：

四輪驅動車只會讓人困在更崎嶇的險地。

▼人生大道定律：

如果大家都衝著你來，那是你走錯方向了。

▼給兒童的相對論：

時間在快速移動的交通工具上過得較慢。

▼Athena 的駕駛禮節法則：

如果你讓別人超你的車，有以下兩種結果：

a. 這輛車一過平交道就有火車，你只得等一列又長又慢的火車開過；或者

b. 你們都去同一個地方，那輛車把僅剩的一個停車位佔走。

▼Lemar 的停車教訓：

如果你必須把車停到六個街口外，你會發現大樓門口就有兩個新的停車位。

▼Karinthy 的定義：

所謂公車，就是走對面車道往相反方向的車。

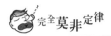

◥McKEE'S LAW:

When you're not in a hurry, the traffic light will turn green as soon as your vehicle comes to a complete stop.

◥GRAY'S LAW FOR BUSES:

A bus that has refused to arrive will do so only when the would-be rider has walked to a point so close to the destination that it is no longer worthwhile to board the bus.

◥QUIGLEY'S LAW:

A car and a truck approaching each other on an otherwise deserted road will meet at the narrow bridge.

◥FIRST LAW OF TRAFFIC:

The slow lane you were stopped in starts moving as soon as you leave it.

◥SECOND LAW OF TRAFFIC:

The extra hour you allowed for traffic will be superseded by an hour-and-a-half traffic jam.

◥REECE'S LAW:

The speed of an oncoming vehicle is directly proportional to the length of the passing zone.

◥MILLER'S LAW OF INSURANCE:

Insurance covers everything except what happens.

◥MILSTEAD'S DRIVING PRINCIPLE:

Whenever you need to stop at a light to put on makeup, every light will be green.

◤McKee 的定律：

　　如果你不急，才把車停住紅綠燈就變綠。

◤Gray 的公車定律：

　　公車老是不來，等到想搭車的人快要走到目的地不用搭車了，車
　　才姍姍來遲。

◤Quigley 的定律：

　　路上要是只有一輛汽車與一輛卡車相向駛來，兩者一定在窄橋碰
　　頭。

◤第一條交通定律：

　　原本那車道要是移動緩慢，你才換車道它就快起來。

◤第二條交通定律：

　　留一個鐘頭當交通時間，就會遇上一個半鐘頭的塞車。

◤Reece 的定律：

　　迎面駛來的車子其速度與交會區的長度成正比。

◤Miller 的保險定律：

　　什麼險都保了，除了出事的那項以外。

◤Milstead 的駕駛原則：

　　想趁紅燈補個妝，就一路綠燈。

◥LOVKA'S LAW OF DRIVING:

There is no traffic until you need to make a left turn.

◥DREW'S LAW OF HIGHWAY BIOLOGY:

The first bug to hit a clean windshield lands directly in front of your eyes.

◥LAW OF HIGHWAY CONSTRUCTION:

The most heavily traveled streets spend the most time under construction.

◥WINFIELD'S DICTUM OF DIRECTION GIVING:

The possibility of getting lost is directly proportional to the number of times the direction-giver says, "You can't miss it."

◥JEAN'S LAW OF AUTOMOTIVES:

Any car utilized as a "back-up" car breaks down just after the primary car breaks down.

▼Lovka 的駕駛定律：
　路上原本都沒車，才要左轉就有車。

▼Drew 的公路生物學定律：
　第一隻撞上擋風玻璃的蟲子，一定撞在你的眼前。

▼公路修建定律：
　交通量最大的路，花最多時間修建。

▼Winfield 的問路格言：
　迷路的機率與人家說「你絕對找的到」的次數成正比。

▼Jean 的汽車定律：
　備用的車子一定在常用的那輛拋錨後也跟著拋
　錨。

完全莫非定律

CAMPBELL'S LAWS OF AUTOMOTIVE REPAIR:

1. If you can get to the faulty part, you don't have the tool to get it off.

2. If you can get the part off, the parts house will have it back-ordered.

3. If it's in stock, it didn't need replacing in the first place.

BROMBERG'S LAWS OF AUTOMOTIVE REPAIR:

1. When the need arises, any tool or object closest to you becomes a hammer.

2. No matter how minor the task, you will inevitably end up covered with grease and motor oil.

3. When necessary, metric and inch tools can be used interchangeably.

FEMO'S LAW OF AUTOMOTIVE ENGINE REPAIRING:

If you drop something, it will never reach the ground.

▼Campbell 的汽車修理定律：

　　1. 找到故障的零件，就沒有拆卸的工具。

　　2. 把故障的零件卸下來了，零件商正好沒貨。

　　3. 如果有貨，原先根本就不必換。

▼Bromberg 的汽車修理定律：

　　1. 有需要的時候，手邊的東西都當鐵槌使用。

　　2. 不管事情多小，都會弄得全身油汙。

　　3. 必要時，公尺制與英尺制的工具可以混用。

▼Femo 的汽車引擎修理定律：

　　不管掉什麼東西，還沒觸地就消失了。

HOUSEHOLD MURPHOLOGY

家庭篇

O'REILLY'S LAW OF THE KITCHEN:

Cleanliness is next to impossible.

ALICE HAMMOND'S LAWS OF THE KITCHEN:

1. Souffles rise and cream whips only for the family and for guests you didn't really want to invite anyway.
2. The rotten egg will be the one you break into the cake batter.
3. Any cooking utensil placed in the dishwasher will be needed immediately thereafter for something else; any measuring utensil used for liquid ingredients will be needed immediately thereafter for dry ingredients.
4. Time spent consuming a meal is in inverse proportion to time spent preparing it.
5. Whatever it is, somebody will have had it for lunch.

THE PARTY LAW:

The more food you prepare, the less your guests eat.

SEVEN LAWS OF KITCHEN CONFUSION:

1. Multiple-function gadgets will not perform any function adequately.

Corollary: The more expensive the gadget, the less often you will use it.

2. The simpler the instructions (e.g.,"Press here"), the more difficult it will be to open the package.
3. In a family recipe you just discovered in an old book, the most vital measurement will be illegible.

Corollary: You will discover that you can't read it only after you have mixed all the other ingredients.

◥O'Reilly 的廚房定律：

別指望有乾淨的一天。

◥Alice Hammond 的廚房定律：

1. 只有為家人或不是真的想邀請的客人所做的酥餅才會鬆、鮮奶
   油才打得發泡。
2. 壞掉的蛋正好是打進蛋奶麵糊的那個。
3. 剛放進洗碗機的廚具，往往馬上就要用到；剛量完液體原料的
   量杯，往往就得用它量乾的原料。
4. 吃一頓飯的時間，與準備的那頓飯的時間成反比。
5. 不管準備什麼菜，總會有人午餐那頓就吃過了。

◥宴會定律：

準備的菜愈多，客人吃得愈少。

◥七條廚房混亂定律：

1. 多功能的小工具，沒有一樣功能管用。
   以此類推：這個東西愈貴你就愈少用。
2. 說明愈簡單（比方說「壓此處」）的包裝愈難打開。
3. 你剛在舊書中找到家傳配方，最要緊的份量卻看不懂寫啥。
   以此類推：你把別的原料都調好了，才發現這裡的字跡看不懂。

4. Once a dish is fouled up, anything added to save it only makes it worse.

5. You are always complimented on the item that took the least effort to prepare.

Example: If you make "duck á l'orange," you will be complimented on the baked potato.

6. The one ingredient you made a special trip to the store to get will be the one thing your guest is allergic to.

7. The more time and energy you put into preparing a meal, the greater the chance your guests will spend the entire meal discussing other meals they have had.

◤WORKING COOK'S LAWS:

1. If you're wondering if you took the meat out to thaw, you didn't.

2. If you're wondering if you left the coffee pot plugged in, you did.

3. If you're wondering if you need to stop and pick up bread and eggs on the way home, you do.

4. If you're wondering if you have enough money to take the family out to eat tonight, you don't.

◤MRS. WEILER'S LAW:

Anything is edible if it is chopped finely enough.

◤FAUSNER'S RULE OF THE HOUSEHOLD:

A knife too dull to cut anything else can always cut your finger.

◤FAUSNER'S DEFINITION:

Housework is what nobody notices unless it's not done.

4. 菜一旦做壞了，再加什麼補救只有更糟。

5. 花最少工夫的菜人家最誇。

例子：如果你做一道柳橙鴨，人家會讚美點綴用的烤馬鈴薯。

6. 特別上街到店裡頭買的原料，就是會讓客人過敏的東西。

7. 一頓飯花的準備時間和工夫愈多，客人就愈可能在餐桌上討論別頓飯局。

▼在職廚師定律：

1. 如果不知道肉有沒有拿出來解凍，一定沒拿。

2. 如果不知道咖啡壺的插頭拔了沒，一定沒拔。

3. 如果不知道在回家路上該不該買麵包和雞蛋，一定該。

4. 如果不知道錢夠不夠帶全家出去上館子，一定不夠。

▼Weiler 太太的定律：

什麼東西切得夠細了都能吃。

▼Fausner 的家事法則：

鈍得什麼都切不動的刀子，就是能割傷你的指頭。

▼Fausner 的說法：

家事這種東西，有做沒人注意，沒做才有人注意。

HAMILTON'S RULE FOR CLEANING GLASSWARE:
The spot you are scrubbing is always on the other side.

Corollary:
If the spot is on the inside, you won't be able to reach it.

YEAGER'S LAW:
Washing machines only break down during the wash cycle.

Corollaries:
1. All breakdowns occur on the plumber's day off.
2. Cost of repair can be determined by multiplying the cost of your new coat by 1.75, or by multiplying the cost of a new washer by .75.

WALKER'S LAW OF THE HOUSEHOLD:
There is always more dirty laundry than clean laundry.

Clive's Rebuttal to Walker's Law:
If it's clean, it isn't laundry.

SKOFF'S LAW:
A child will not spill on a dirty floor.

WITZLING'S LAWS OF PROGENY PERFORMANCE:
1. Any child who chatters nonstop at home will adamantly refuse to utter a word when requested to demonstrate for an audience.
2. Any shy, introverted child will choose a crowded public area to loudly demonstrate newly acquired vocabulary (damn, penis, etc.).

O'TOOLE'S AXIOM:
One child is not enough, but two children are far too many.

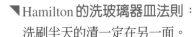

Hamilton 的洗玻璃器皿法則：
洗刷半天的漬一定在另一面。

以此類推：
如果漬在內側，一定刷不到。

Yeager 的定律：
洗衣機只在洗衣功能那段才會壞。

以此類推：
1. 故障一定挑水管工人的休息日。
2. 修理成本可以這麼算：把新外套的價格乘以 1.75，或者把新洗碗機的價格乘以 0.75。

Walker 的家事定律：
還沒送洗的髒衣物，總是比送洗好的乾淨衣物多。

Clive 反駁 Walker 的定律：
乾淨的就無所謂送洗。

Skoff 的定律：
兒童在髒地板上不會打翻東西。

Witzling 的子女行為定律：
1. 在家裡咶噪不休的孩子，要他對一群人說話就死也不肯開口。
2. 害羞內向的孩子都會找個人群擁擠的公開場合，大聲示範新學來的詞彙（像是「幹」、「陰莖」等）。

O'Toole 的格言：
小孩一個嫌少，兩個又太多。

◤VAN ROY'S LAW:

An unbreakable toy is useful for breaking other toys.

◤H. FISH'S LAWS OF ANIMAL BEHAVIOR:

1. The probability of a cat eating its dinner has absolutely nothing to do with the price of the food placed before it.
2. The probability that a household pet will raise a fuss to go in or out is directly proportional to the number and importance of your dinner guests.

◤THE PET PRINCIPLE:

No matter which side of the door the dog or cat is on, it is the wrong side.

◤RULE OF FELINE FRUSTRATION:

When your cat has fallen asleep on your lap and looks utterly content and adorable, you will suddenly have to go to the bathroom.

▼Van Roy 的定律：

打不壞的玩具正好用來打壞其他玩具。

▼H. Fish 的動物行為定律：

1. 貓吃不吃晚餐，跟你爲牠準備的晚餐有多貴一點關係也沒有。

2. 寵物會不會吵著要進來或出去，跟來訪客人的人數與重要程度
   有絕對關係。

▼寵物原則：

不管貓狗在門的哪一邊，一定是錯的那邊。

▼貓族沮喪法則：

要是你的貓在你的腿上睡著了，模樣既滿足又
可愛，你就忽然想上廁所。

BOREN'S LAW FOR CATS:

When in doubt, wash.

FISKE'S TEENAGE COROLLARY TO PARKINSON'S LAW:

The stomach expands to accommodate the amount of junk food available.

BANANA PRINCIPLE:

If you buy bananas or avocados before they are ripe, there won't be any left by the time they are ripe. If you buy them ripe, they rot before they are eaten.

BALLANCE'S LAW OF RELATIVITY:

How long a minute is depends on which side of the bathroom door you're on.

BRITT'S GREEN THUMB POSTULATE:

The life expectancy of a house plant varies inversely with its price and directly with its ugliness.

MARQUETTE'S FIRST LAW OF HOME REPAIR:

The tool you need is just out of reach.

MARQUETTE'S SECOND LAW OF HOME REPAIR:

The first replacement part you buy will be the wrong size.

MARQUETTE'S THIRD LAW OF HOME REPAIR:

A lost tool will be found immediately upon purchasing a new one.

MALONE'S LAW OF THE HOUSEHOLD:

If you wait all day for the repairman, you'll wait all day. If you go out for five minutes, he'll arrive and leave while you're gone.

▉Boren 的養貓定律：
有問題就洗。

▉Fiske 的青少年類推 Parkinson 的定律：
垃圾食物有多少，胃就變多大。

▉香蕉原則：
如果買生的香蕉或鱷梨，沒等熟就吃光了。如果買熟的，沒等吃
就爛了。

▉Ballance 的相對論定律：
一分鐘有多長，要看你在廁所的裡頭或外頭。

▉Britt 的園藝假設：
室內植物的存活力跟價格成反比，跟醜度成正比。

▉Marquette 的家庭修繕第一定律：
需要的工具正好就在搆不著的地方。

▉Marquette 的家庭修繕第二定律：
最先買的替換零件，尺寸一定不對。

▉Marquette 的家庭修繕第三定律：
買了新的工具，不見的就立刻找到。

▉Malone 的家事定律：
如果花整天等修理工人，他整天都不來。才離
開五分鐘，工人正好就來了又走掉。

MINTON'S LAW OF PAINTING:

Any paint, no matter what the quality or composition, will adhere permanently to any surface if applied accidentally.

LAWS OF GARDENING:

1. Other people's tools work only in other people's gardens.
2. Fancy gizmos don't work.
3. If nobody uses it, there's a reason.
4. You get the most of what you need the least.

KITMAN'S LAW:

Pure drivel tends to drive ordinary drivel off the TV Screen.

LAW OF RERUNS:

If you have watched a TV series only once, and you watch it again, it will be a rerun of the same episode.

▼Minton 的粉刷定律：
不管是什麼質地或成份的漆，不小心沾到任何表面都清不掉。

▼園藝定律：
1. 別人的工具只在別人的花園有用。
2. 花俏的玩意沒用。
3. 沒人用的一定有問題。
4. 最不需要的買最多。

▼Kitman 的定律：
電視上頭的言不及義，最後都敗給不知所云。

▼重播定律：
如果有部電視影集你只看過一次，看重播時，
播的還是你看過的那集。

◥JONES' LAW OF TV PROGRAMMING:

1. If there are only two shows worth watching, they will be on at the same time.
2. The only new show worth watching will be cancelled.
3. The show you're been looking forward to all week will be preempted.

◥BESS UNIVERSAL PRINCIPLES:

1. The telephone will ring when you are outside the door, fumbling for your keys.
2. You will reach it just in time to hear the click of the caller hanging up.

◥KOVAC'S CONUNDRUM:

When you dial a wrong number, you never get a busy signal.

◥BELL'S THEOREM:

When a body is immersed in water, the telephone rings.

◥RYAN'S APPLICATION OF PARKINSON'S LAW:

Possessions increase to fill the space available for their storage.

◥RINGWALD'S LAW OF HOUSEHOLD GEOMETRY:

Any horizontal surface is soon piled up.

◥THE PINEAPPLE PRINCIPLE:

The best parts of anything are always impossible to separate from the inedible parts.

◥LAW OF SUPERMARKETS:

The quality of the house brand varies inversely with the size of the supermarket chain.

▼Jones 的電視節目定律：
  1. 如果只有兩個節目值得看，就會同時間播。
  2. 唯一值得看的新節目會停播。
  3. 盼了一整週的節目會提前播。

▼Bess 的通則：
  1. 你在門外翻鑰匙，電話就會響。
  2. 等你接了，正好聽到對方卡一聲掛斷。

▼Kovac 的疑惑：
  撥錯號碼時，對方一定不是通話中。

▼Bell 的理則：
  才泡進澡盆電話就響。

▼Ryan 應用 Parkinson 的定律：
  儲藏空間有多少，東西就有多少。

▼Ringwald 的家事幾何學定律：
  任何水平表面沒幾天便會堆起東西。

▼鳳梨原則：
  只要是精華，總是跟不能吃的部份分不開。

▼超市定律：
  超市愈大，自製品牌的品質愈差。

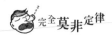

◣LAW OF SUPERMARKET SHOPPING:

The longer the shopping list, the more likely it will be left at home.

◣THE GROCERY BAG LAW:

The candy bar you planned to eat on the way home from the market will be at the bottom of the grocery bag.

◣WOODSIDE'S GROCERY PRINCIPLE:

The bag that breaks is the one with the eggs.

◣ESTHER'S LAW:

The fussiest person will be the one to get the chipped coffee cup, the glass with lipstick, or the hair in the food.

◣POPE'S LAW:

Chipped dishes never break.

◣HOROWITZ'S LAW:

Whenever you turn on the radio, you hear the last few notes of your favorite song.

▼超市購物定律：
　想買的東西愈多，愈可能把清單忘在家裡。

▼購物袋定律：
　打算在回家路上吃的糖果零食，一定放在袋子的底部。

▼Woodside 的雜貨原則：
　破掉的袋子一定是裝蛋的那個。

▼Esther 的定律：
　最愛吹毛求疵的人，就會拿到有裂縫的咖啡杯、有口紅印的玻璃杯、有頭髮的食物。

▼Pope 的定律：
　有裂縫的盤子就是不破。

▼Horowitz 的定律：
　每次打開收音機，就會聽到心愛的歌快唱完了。

◤ZELMAN'S RULE OF RADIO RECEPTION:

Your pocket radio won't pick up the station you want to hear most.

◤GERARD'S LAW:

When there are sufficient funds in the checking account, checks take two weeks to clear. When there are insufficient funds, checks clear overnight.

◤SEYMOUR'S INVESTMENT PRINCIPLE:

Never invest in anything that eats.

▼Zelman 的收音法則：

口袋型收音機總收不到你最想聽的電台。

▼Gerard 的定律：

帳戶裡有足夠的錢，支票要兩週才到期。帳戶裡錢不夠了，支票明天就到期。

▼Seymour 的投資原則：

千萬別投資在需要食物的東西上。

CONSUMEROLOGY AND SALESMANSHIP

消費與推銷篇

HERBLOCK'S LAW:

If it's good, they discontinue it.

GOLD'S LAW:

If the shoe fits, it's ugly.

HADLEY'S LAWS OF CLOTHES SHOPPING:

1. If you like it, they don't have it in your size.
2. If you like it and they have it in your size, it doesn't fit anyway.
3. If you like it and it fits, you can't afford it.
4. If you like it, it fits and you can afford it, it falls apart the first time you wear it.

FINMAN'S BARGAIN BASEMENT PRINCIPLE:

The one you want is never the one on sale.

Baker's Corollary:

You never want the one you can afford.

LEWIS' LAW:

No matter how long or how hard you shop for an item, after you've bought it, it will be on sale somewhere cheaper.

HERSHISER'S RULES:

1. Anything labeled "NEW" and/or "IMPROVED" isn't.
2. The label "NEW" and/or "IMPROVED" means the price went up.
3. The label "ALL NEW," "COMPLETELY NEW" or "GREAT NEW" means the price went way up.

McGOWAN'S MADISON AVENUE AXIOM:

If an item is advertised as "under $50," you can bet it's not $19.95.

Herblock 的定律：
東西好就不再賣了。

Gold 的定律：
鞋合腳就醜。

Hadley 的購衣定律：
1. 喜歡就沒有你的尺寸。
2. 喜歡也有尺寸卻不合身。
3. 喜歡也合身卻買不起。
4. 喜歡也合身又買得起，卻第一次穿就裂開。

Finman 的大拍賣原則：
你要的一定沒打折。

Baker 的類推：
你從來不會想買你買得起的東西。

Lewis 的定律：
不管花多久時間、多少工夫到處比價，才買了就會有個地方以更低的價格拍賣。

Hershiser 的法則：
1. 「新產品」和（或）「加強功能」等標籤是真的才怪。
2. 「新產品」和（或）「加強功能」等標籤的意思是
   價格漲了。
3. 貼了「全新產品」、「最新產品」、「超新產品」等標籤，價格
   更是飛漲。

McGowan 的麥迪遜大道格言：
要是廣告說「50 元有找」，你可以保證不會是
19.95 元。

◥ LAW OF THE MARKETPLACE:

If only one price can be obtained for any quotation, the price will be unreasonable.

◥ SECOND LAW OF THE MARKETPLACE:

Weekend specials aren't.

◥ PANTUSO'S LAW:

The book you spent $29.95 for today will come out in paperback tomorrow.

◥ GLASER'S LAW:

If it says "one size fits all", it doesn't fit anyone.

◥ RILEY'S "*MURPHY'S LAW*" LAWS:

1. Stores that sell Volume One will not know of Volume Two.
2. Stores that sell Volume Two will be out of Volume One.

◥ VILE'S LAW OF VALUE:

The more an item costs, the farther you have to send it for repairs.

◥ MURRAY'S LAWS:

1. Never ask a barber if you need a haircut.
2. Never ask a salesman if his is a good price.

◥ GOLDENSTERN'S RULES:

1. Always hire a rich attorney.
2. Never buy from a rich salesperson.

◥ SINTETOS' LAW OF CONSUMERISM:

A sixty-day warranty guarantees that the product will self-destruct on the sixty-first day.

市場定律：

報價要是只有一種價格，這個價格一定不便宜。

市場定律第二條：

週末特賣品絕不特別。

Pantuso 的定律：

今天花 29.95 元美金買精裝書，明天就有平裝版可買。

Glaser 的定律：

單一尺碼的衣服，誰穿都不合身。

Riley 的《莫非定律》定律：

1. 賣第一冊的店沒聽過有第二冊。
2. 賣第二冊的店，第一冊賣完了。

Vile 的價值定律：

一樣東西愈貴，維修就得送得愈遠。

Murray 的定律：

1. 千萬別問理髮師頭髮需不需要剪。
2. 千萬別問推銷員價格便不便宜。

Goldenstern 的法則：

1. 律師一定得找有錢的。
2. 別跟有錢的推銷員買東西。

Sintetos 的消費主義定律：

保用六十天的產品，保證在第六十一天自動毀滅。

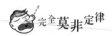

BERYL'S LAW:

The Consumer Report article on the item will come out a week after you're made your purchase.

Corollaries:

1. The one you bought will be rated "unacceptable."
2. The one you almost bought will be rated "best buy."

SAVIGNANO'S MAIL-ORDER LAW:

If you don't write to complain, you'll never receive your order.

If you do write, you'll receive the merchandise before your angry letter reaches its destination.

YOUNT'S LAWS OF MAIL ORDERING:

1. The most important item in an order will no longer be available.
2. The next most important item will be back-ordered for six months.
3. During the time an item is back-ordered, it will be available more cheaply and quickly from many other sources.
4. As soon as a back-order has entered the no longer available category, the item will "no longer be obtainable anywhere" at any price.

LEWIS' LAW:

People will buy anything that's one to a customer.

BROOKS' LAW OF RETAILING:

Security isn't.

Management can't.

Sales promotions don't.

Consumer assistance doesn't.

Workers won't.

▼Beryl 的定律：

　　東西買了以後一週，《消費者報導》就會討論這樣東西。

▼以此類推：

　　1. 已經買了的會列入「不及格」類。

　　2. 差點買了的會列入「最佳選擇」類。

▼Savignano 的郵購定律：

　　如果不投函抱怨，貨永遠不來。

　　當真寫了，滿紙怒氣的信還沒到人家那兒，東西就來了。

▼Yount 的郵購定律：

　　1. 訂單裡最重要的一項沒貨了。

　　2. 第二重要的貨要等六個月才有。

　　3. 在等貨期間，就有許多地方都有更便宜、更快的貨源。

　　4. 等到訂購中的貨列入「無法取得」一欄，到哪裡、出什麼價都

　　　　買不到。

▼Lewis 的定律：

　　一人限買一件的東西大家搶著買。

▼Brooks 的零售商定律：

　　保全不安全。

　　管理無能。

　　促銷不賣。

　　客戶服務不週。

　　員工不幹活。

COSMO-MURPHOLOGY
莫非通則篇

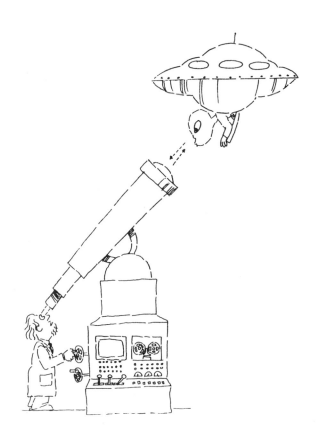

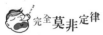

◥OLIVIER'S LAW:

Experience is something you don't get until just after you need it.

◥LAW OF LIVING:

As soon as you're doing what you wanted to be doing, you want to be doing something else.

◥FIRST RULE OF PATHOLOGY:

Most well-trodden paths lead nowhere.

◥GABITOL'S OBSERVATION:

The wise are pleased when they discover truth, fools when they discover falsehood.

◥FOSTER'S LAW:

The only people who find what they are looking for in life are the fault-finders.

◥FIRST RULE OF NEGATIVE ANTICIPATION:

You will save yourself a lot of needless worry if you don't burn your bridges until you come to them.

◥FIRST PRINCIPLE OF SELF-DETERMINATION:

What you resist, you become.

◥STEINER'S PRECEPTS:

1. Knowledge based on external evidence is unreliable.
2. Logic can never decide what is possible or impossible.

◥COLRIDGE'S LAW:

Extremes meet.

◥FEINBERG'S PRINCIPLE:

Memory serves its own master.

▼Olivier 的定律：
　經驗這種東西，需要的時機剛過才來。

▼生活定律：
　才做想做的事，就想做別的事。

▼第一條「道」的法則：
　人群往來的路走不到哪去。

▼Gabitol 的心得：
　智者因發現眞理而高興，愚人則因揭穿假象。

▼Foster 的定律：
　只有吹毛求疵的人，才找得到自己人生中想找的東西。

▼第一條負面期望法則：
　過河再拆橋，可以省你很多麻煩。

▼第一條自決原則：
　怕什麼就變成什麼。

▼Steiner 的前題：
　1. 以外在證據爲依據的知識不可靠。
　2. 邏輯永遠無法決定什麼事可能發生，什麼事不可能。

▼Colridge 的定律：
　物極必反。

▼Feinberg 的原則：
　記憶滿足回憶的人。

VOLTAIRE'S LAW:

There is nothing more respectable than an ancient evil.

LAST LAW OF ROBOTICS:

The only real errors are human errors.

HOFFER'S LAW:

When people are free to do as they please, they usually imitate each other.

BERRA'S FIRST LAW:

You can observe a lot just by watching.

BERRA'S SECOND LAW:

Anyone who is popular is bound to be disliked.

PERLSWEIG'S LAW:

Whatever goes around, comes around.

MEADOW'S MAXIM:

You can't push on a rope.

OPPENHEIMER'S LAW:

There is no such thing as instant experience.

DISIMONI'S RULE OF COGNITION:

Believing is seeing.

THE SIDDHARTHA PRINCIPLE:

You cannot cross a river in two strides.

KIERKEGAARD'S OBSERVATION:

Life can only be understood backwards, but it must be lived

▼伏爾泰（18世紀法國文豪）的定律：
　遠古的惡魔最可敬。

▼最後一條機械人定律：
　真正的錯誤是人為錯誤。

▼Hoffer 的定律：
　人有機會隨心所欲時，往往彼此模仿。

▼第一條 Berra 的定律：
　光看就會有許多心得。

▼第二條 Berra 的定律：
　萬人迷一定討人厭。

▼Perlsweig 的定律：
　該來的就會來。

▼Meadow 的格言：
　繩子不能用推的。

▼歐本海默（原子彈之父）的定律：
　天底下沒有速成的經驗。

▼Disimoni 的理解法則：
　相信就會看見。

▼佛陀原則：
　河不是兩三步過得了的。

▼齊克果（丹麥哲學家）的心得：
　人生要回頭看才能理解，但日子卻得往前走。

METALAWS
超定律

LES MISERABLES METALAW:

All laws, whether good, bad or indifferent, must be obeyed to the letter.

PERSIG'S POSTULATE:

The number of rational hypotheses that can explain any given phenomenon is infinite.

LILLY'S METALAW:

All laws are simulations of reality.

THE ULTMATE PRINCIPLE:

By definition, when you are investigating the unknown you do not know what you will find.

COOPER'S METALAW:

A proliferation of new laws creates a proliferation of new loopholes.

DIGIOVANNI'S LAW:

The number of laws will expand to fill the publishing space available.

LEO ROGERS' BLESSING FOR VOLUME II:

If it's worth doing, it's worth overdoing.

ROGERS' OBSERVATION REGARDING THE LAWS:

In a bureaucratic hierarchy, the higher up in the organization you go, the less people appreciate Murphy's Law, the Peter Principle, etc.

◤《悲慘世界》的超定律：
一切定律，不管好、壞、公正與否，都必須一個字母一個字母照做。

◤Persig 的假設：
任何現有的現象都有無數個合情理的假設。

◤Lilly 的超定律：
一切定律都是現實的模擬。

◤終極原則：
就定義而言，研究未來的東西，你不會知道結果會是什麼。

◤Cooper 的超定律：
大量的新定律帶來大量的新漏洞。

◤Digiovanni 的定律：
版面有多少，定律就有多少。

◤Leo Rogers 給第二冊的祝福：
值得做的事，就值得做過頭。

◤Rogers 的定律心得：
在官僚階級體系裡，爬得愈高，愈少人欣賞莫非定律、彼得原則等等。

◥OAK'S PRINCIPLES OF LAW-MAKING:

1. Law expands in proportion to the resources available for its enforcement.
2. Bad law is more likely to be supplemented than repealed.
3. Social legislation cannot repeal physical laws.

◥JAFFE'S PRECEPT:

There are some things that are impossible to know—but it is impossible to know these things.

◥MUIR'S LAW:

When we try to pick out anything by itself, we find it hitched to everything else in the universe.

◥MIKSCH'S LAW:

If a string has one end, then it has another end.

◥COLE'S LAW:

Thinly sliced cabbage.

◥DUCHARM'S AXIOM:

If one views one's problem closely enough, one will recognize oneself as part of the problem.

◥LAW OF ARBITRARY DISTINCTION:

Anything may be divided into as many parts as you please.

◥Corollary:

Everything may be divided into as many parts as you please.

▼Oak 的定律編纂原則：

1. 支持定律的證據愈多，定律變得愈長。

2. 不好的定律加以補充的機會大，撤銷的機會小。

3. 社會立法無法撤銷物理定律。

▼Jaffe 的箴言：

有些事情不可能了解——不過你不可能知道是哪些。

▼Muir 的定律：

要是想把某個東西單獨挑出來，就會發現那樣東西跟宇宙裡的一切都有牽連。

▼Miksch 的定律：

總是有一端就會有另一端。

▼花菜定律：

切細的高麗菜（Cole slaw 指高麗菜沙拉，與 Cole's Law 只差一點）。

▼Ducharm 的格言：

大家如果仔細研究問題，就會發現自己也是問題的一部分。

▼隨意區分定律：

無論什麼事情你愛分成幾部分，就可以分成幾部分。

▼以此類推：

所有的事情你愛分成幾部分，就可以分成幾部分。

◥Commentary on the Corollary:

In this case, "everything" may be viewed as a subset of "anything."

◥WALLACE'S OBSERVATION:

Everything is in a state of utter dishevelment.

◥WELWOOD'S AXIOM:

Disorder expands proportionately to the tolerance for it.

◥HARTLEY'S SECOND LAW:

You can lead a horse to water, but if you can get him to float on his back, you're got something.

◥FOWLER'S NOTE:

The only imperfect thing in nature is the human race.

◥TRISCHMANN'S PARADOX:

A pipe gives a wise man time to think and a fool something to stick in his mouth.

◥CHURCHILL'S COMMENTARY ON MAN:

Man will occasionally stumble over the truth, but most of the time he will pick himself up and continue on.

◥HALDANE'S LAW:

The universe is not only queerer than we imagine, it's queerer than we can imagine.

◥LAW OF OBSERVATION:

Nothing looks as good close up as it does from far away.
Or—nothing looks as good from far away as it does close up.

▼對上條以此類推的評論：

這樣的話，「所有的事情」可以視爲「無論什麼事情」的子集合。

▼Wallace 的心得：

什麼東西都亂七八糟。

▼Welwood 的格言：

髒亂與容忍成正比。

▼Hartley 的第二定律：

把馬帶到水邊不難，可是能教牠仰漂就得有兩把刷子。

▼Fowler 的註腳：

大自然唯一的瑕疵是人類。

▼Trischmann 的反論：

抽煙斗讓智者有時間思考，讓愚人有個東西塞嘴巴。

▼邱吉爾（英國前首相）評人類：

人類誤打誤撞碰到眞理，不過多半爬起來又走開。

▼Haldane 的定律：

宇宙之奇我們沒想到，也不是我們想得到的。

▼觀察定律：

東西遠看美，近看就沒那麼美了。

或者說——東西近看美，遠看就沒那麼美了。

THE AQUINAS AXIOM:

What the gods get away with, the cows don't.

NEWTON'S LITTLE-KNOWN SEVENTH LAW:

A bird in the hand is safer than one overhead.

WHITE'S CHAPPAQUIDDICK THEOREM:

The sooner and in more detail you announce the bad news, the better.

THE LAST LAW:

If several things that could have gone wrong have not gone wrong, it would have been ultimately beneficial for them to have gone wrong.

MATSCH'S LAW:

It's better to have a horrible ending than to have horrors without end.

神學家的話：
眾神逃掉的，牛逃不掉。

罕為人知的牛頓第七定律：
鳥在手上的比在頭頂上保險。

White 的 Chappaquiddick 定理：
壞消息宣佈得愈早、愈詳細愈好（Chappaquiddick 事件是美國政治史上的醜聞案）。

最後定律：
幾件該出錯的事要是沒出錯，那麼這幾件事要是出錯了，最後一定有好處。

Matsch 的定律：
恐怖的結局勝過恐怖而沒有結局。

ACKNOWLEDGMENTS AND PERMISSIONS
誌謝與授權

Grateful acknowledgment is made to the following for permission to reprint their material:

"Datamation." *Laws of Computer Programming.* Greenwich, Connecticut: Technical Publishing Co., 1968.

"Spark's Ten Rules for the Project Manager" ; "Laws of Procrastination" ; "Gordon's First Law" ; "Maier's Law" ; "Edington's Theory" ; "Parkinson's Law for Medical Research" ; "Peter's Hidden Postulate According to Godin" ; "Godin's Law" ; "Freeman's Rule" ; "Old and Kahn's Law" ; "First Law of Socio-Genetics" ; "Hersh's Law." *Journal of Irreproducible Results.* Box 234, Chicago Heights, Illinois.

Parkinson, C. Northcote. "Parkinson's First, Second, Third, Fourth and Fifth Laws" ; "Parkinson's Law of Delay" ; "Parkinson's Axioms." *Parkinson's Law, Mrs. Parkinson's Law, The Law and the Profits, The Law of Delay and In-Laws and Outlaws.* Boston: Houghton Mifflin Company.

Peter, Dr. Laurence J. and Raymond Hull. "The Peter Principle and Its Corollaries: Peter's Inversion; Peter's Placebo; Peter's Prognosis; Peter's Law of Evolution*; Peter's Observation*; Peter's Law of Substitution*; Peter's Rule for Creative Incompetence*; Peter's Theorem.*" *The Peter Principle.* New York: William Morrow and Co., 1969.

(*so named by the editors)

"Matz's Laws, Mottos, etc." ; "Barach's Rule" ; "Bernstein's Precept" ; "Cochrane's Aphorism" ; "Lord Cohen's Comment" ; "Loeb's Laws of Medicine" ; "Shumway's Law." *New York State Journal of Medicine*, copyright by the Medical Society of the State of New York, "Principles of Medicine,"

(Jan. 1977) and "More Principles of Medicine," (Oct. 1977) by Robert Matz, M.D.

Shedenhelm, W.R.C. "Shedenhelm's Laws of Backpacking." *The Backpacker's Guide*. Mountain View: World Publications, 1979.

Block, Herbert, "Herblock's Law." *Herblock's State of the Union*. New york: Simon & Schuster, 1972.

Alinsky, Saul. "Alinsky's Rule for Radicals." *Rules for Radicals.* New York: Random House, Inc., 1971.

"Kamin's Law." *L.A. Herald Examiner.* Dec. 2, 1973.

"Glogg's Law." *National Review.* (150 East 35th St., New York, NY, 10016), Mar. 29, 1974.

Block, Arthur. "Four Workshop Principles" ; "Five Laws of Office Murphology" ; "Eight Laws of Kitchen Confusion" ; "Laws of Class Scheduling" ; "Laws of Applied Terror." *Murphy's Law(s) Plaques for the Workshop; for the Office; for the Kitchen; for Students*. Los Angeles: Price Stern Sloan, Inc., 1978.

"Borkowski's Law" ; "Hart's Law of Observation" ; "Law of Probable Dispersal." *Verbatim.* 1977.

Gall, John, M.D. "Systematics." *How Systems Work and Especially How They Fail.* New York: Times Books, 1977.

"Hofstedt's Law" ; "Horngren's Observation" ; "MacDonald's First and Second Laws." *Alumni Bulletin.* Stanford School of Business, Vol. 46, No. 3. Copyright 1978 by the Board of Trustees of Leland Stanford Junior University. All rights reserved.

"Ballance's Law of Relativity" ; "Ballance's Law of Pragmatic Passion." *Bill Ballance's Hip Handbook of Nifty Moves.* North Hollywood, California: Melvin Powers-Wilshire Book Co.

Reed, Fred. "The Guppy Law." *The Washington Post.* June 27, 1978.

Price, Roger. "Price's Laws." *The Great Roob Revolution.* New York: Random

House, Inc., 1970.

"Telesco's Laws of Nursing." *American Journal of Nursing.* Dec. 1978, Vol. 78, No. 12.

"Thumb's First and Second Postulates." *Nuclear News.* Aug. 1971.

Hammond, Alice. "Laws of the Kitchen" ; "Working Cooks Laws" ; "Cooper's Rule for Copying Recipes." *Randolph Guide and Greensboro Record.* Mar. 8, 1978.

"Law of Revelation" ; "Evans' Law." *Dukengineer.* October, 1974.

Murray, Jim. "Murray's Rules of the Arena." *L.A. Times.* Nov. 23, 1978.

Smith, Jack. "Dedera's Law." *L.A. Times.* Nov. 10, 1976.

"Byrne's Law of Concreting." *Western Construction.* May 1978.

"Golomb's Don'ts of Mathematical Modelintg." *Astronautics and Aeronautics.* American Institute of Astronautics and Aeronautics. January 1968.

"Finnigan's Law." *Organic Gardening.* June 1978.

Fox, Joe. "Disraeli's Dictum" ; "Wilkie's Law" ; "Things That Can Be Counted on in a Crisis." *Trapped in the Organization.* Los Angeles: Price Stern Sloan, Inc., 1980.

"The Lippman Lemma." *The Worm Runner's Digest.* Vol. 21, No. 1. 1979.

Lowe, Frances. "Lowe's Law." *Lubbock Avalanche-Journal.* January 28, 1979.

Macbeth's Comment on Evolution: "*Towards,*" 17417 Vintage St., Northridge, CA, 91325, Vol. 2, No. 2.

Caen, Herb. "Olivier's Law." "Seeger's Law." *San Francisco Chronicle.* Nov. 29, 1981.

Roche, John P. "Roche's Fifth Law." *Albany Times-Union.* July 14, 1978.

Schrank, Robert. "Schrank's First Law." *Ten Thousand Working Days.* Cambridge, MA: MIT Press, 1978.

Very special thanks also to Conrad Schneiker for his invaluable assistance and support.